# WILD CARD

RENEE ROSE

BURNING DESIRES

**Copyright © December 2019 Wild Card by Renee Rose**

All rights reserved. This copy is intended for the original purchaser of this book ONLY. No part of this book may be reproduced, scanned, or distributed in any printed or electronic form without prior written permission from the author. Please do not participate in or encourage piracy of copyrighted materials in violation of the author's rights. Purchase only authorized editions.

Published in the United States of America

Renee Rose Romance

Editor: Maggie Ryan

This book is a work of fiction. While reference might be made to actual historical events or existing locations, the names, characters, places and incidents are either the product of the author's imaginations or are used fictitiously, and any resemblance to actual persons, living or dead, business establishments, events, or locales is entirely coincidental.

This book contains descriptions of many BDSM and sexual practices, but this is a work of fiction and, as such, should not be used in any way as a guide. The author and publisher will not be responsible for any loss, harm, injury, or death resulting from use of the information contained within. In other words, don't try this at home, folks!

ACKNOWLEDGMENTS

Thank you to Maggie Ryan for her edits and to Aubrey Cara for beta read!

All my love to the Romper Roomies. If you're not a member of my Facebook group, please send me an email at reneeroseauthor@gmail.com to join!

## WANT FREE RENEE ROSE BOOKS?

Click here to sign up for Renee Rose's newsletter and receive a free copy of *Theirs to Protect, Owned by the Marine*, *Theirs to Punish, The Alpha's Punishment, Disobedience at the Dressmaker's* and *Her Billionaire Boss*. In addition to the free stories, you will also get special pricing, exclusive previews and news of new releases.

## CHAPTER 1

*Caitlin*

FISTS AT BOOB LEVEL, elbows back, I lead my dance cardio class through some booty shaking to the song, *Sweet but Psycho*.

Yeah, it's pretty much my theme song.

"Step touch, throw your hand down in front," I sing into the headset, exaggerating the movements to help the class follow along.

Dance cardio is my jam. I teach it four nights a week at the campus rec center and take other movement classes on the off-nights. Anything to keep me moving, which probably seems strange for a computer science geek.

It does border on obsessive, but it's not one of those body-hatred kind of things. I'm not working out to achieve some body ideal or to look a certain way.

I just need to move. I have a hard time staying in my body, otherwise.

*Dissociative disorder* is the official diagnosis. I check out when things get intense for me. Movement helps. Pain and sex work even better.

General consensus—I'm broken.

But that doesn't matter much, because my time is running out.

The siphon I put on the Tacone family's casino business—the one where I skimmed a fifth of a penny from every transaction—got shut down two weeks ago.

And even though I used an off-shore account for storing the funds before they paid for my brother's and my college tuition, there's a decent chance I'm going to end up swimming with the fishes, as they say.

But I knew that going into my little revenge scheme.

"Wide second position, deep breath in." I start the cool down. It's always over too soon. I lead the class through the closing stretches and thank them all for coming.

"Thank you, Caitlin." My students wave and smile as they leave. Here, I'm almost normal. I could be just like any of them. A pretty, wide-smiling graduate student getting her workout.

It's when people get to know me a little better they see my crazy. Decide I'm the girl to give a wide berth around. Which is totally fine with me.

I grab my towel and head to the showers, picking up my phone to check messages. Not that I ever have any. It's just an anxious habit from when my brother Trevor was still in foster care, and I would freak out if he didn't contact me every day to let me know he was still alive.

Still okay. Not living the nightmare I'd lived.

It's one of the many quirks I have the Tacones to thank for. The side effect of having a dad murdered by the mob.

Except now that I've had my revenge, now that they're coming for me, I'm thinking I shouldn't have stirred the hornet's nest.

I was probably better use to Trevor alive than dead. Even if I did generate enough funds to pay our college tuition.

I'd better warn him. I dial his number and he picks right up.

"Hey, Caitie." He's the only person I let call me that.

"Hey, Trevor. Everything okay?"

"Yeah. Why wouldn't it be?" It's sometimes weird to me how normal he turned out compared to me. But he had a decent foster family. And he had me.

I had only ugliness and myself to rely on.

"Hey, I have to tell you something, but it's going to be fine," I say quickly, just to get the words out. I've tried to tell him four other times since the money got cut off, but chickened out every time.

"What is it?"

"Um, I may have hacked a company I shouldn't have messed with."

"Oh shit. What happened? Are you in jail?"

"Nope, not jail. It probably won't go that route. Do you remember who killed Dad?"

Trevor goes dead quiet. When he speaks, his voice sounds scared. "Tell me you didn't."

"I did. Anyway, they probably won't figure it out, but

if they do, you remember the place we used to say we'd meet up if anything bad happened with foster care?"

I don't know why I'm speaking in code. It's not like the mafia are in the locker room right now. Or bugging my phone.

"I remember."

"If I have to run, that's where I'll go. Okay?"

"Shit, Caitie. This is bad. Are you crazy?"

"That's what they say," I remind him in a sing-song voice. "Anyway, nothing's going to happen. I thought I should tell you just in case."

"Maybe you should go hide there now."

"No, I don't even know if they'll trace it to me. But if they do, I'll figure it out. I don't want you to worry."

"Yeah, I'm definitely worried."

My chest warms. Trevor's the only good in my life.

"Well, don't. You know me—I can take care of myself. I'll figure it out. Just be cautious about any texts from me and don't give up my location if anyone comes asking."

"I won't. Shit, Caitlin."

"It's okay. I promise. I'll text you tomorrow."

"All right. Be careful."

"I will." I hang up and shove my phone down in my bag before I strip out of my sweaty clothes and step in the shower.

If only I believed I have this all under control.

I rinse off with the *Sweet but Psycho* song on repeat in my head.

*Paolo*

I BREAK into the apartment of Caitlin—aka *WYLDE*—West using the key I had made by a locksmith who owed me a favor. I sent one of my henchmen over to watch her for the past week and give me the deets on her habits, so I know she's teaching her dance cardio class now.

I know she'll be home soon, and I'm looking forward to putting the surprise on her when she arrives.

Intimidation is an art form I've spent a lifetime perfecting, and I'm going to scare the piss out of the little hacker who targeted my family's casino coffers.

As the second son of now imprisoned Don Tacone, head of the biggest Chicago crime family, I learned how to crack my knuckles and posture practically as a toddler. How to give a beatdown by age six.

Most of the time, my reputation and the flash of a gun do all the work necessary. It's rare I have to actually hurt anyone or make a plain threat.

So when my brother asked me to take care of our hacker, I was happy to do it. Especially after I saw a picture of the computer geek. The moniker Wylde seems to fit her. It's not the mess of long thick hair or black glasses. It's the pink lip gloss on her smirking mouth that makes me think she's not the antisocial nerd you might expect of someone with her exceptional skills.

The place is tiny—a studio, I guess they call it—with the kitchen on one wall and the bed on the other and a tiny bathroom off the living / dining section. It's a mess. Clothes everywhere. Dirty dishes on every surface.

I pick up a miniscule white thong with one finger.

Nerds in hot panties. That could be a whole fetish. Kinda goes with the sexy librarian thing. I toss the panties in her hamper and continue my perusal.

Stacks of books and computer equipment line the walls and desk. An old bike is parked against one wall, helmet hanging from the handlebar.

I wander around, looking through her things. Ramen and baked beans in the cupboards. Frozen burritos in the freezer. At least she's not living large on our cash.

According to my brother, Stefano, all the stolen money was transferred from an off-shore account straight to the bursar's office of Northwestern University. But if I'm supposed to think it's noble that she only steals for her education, I don't. She fucked with the wrong family.

I stop to examine her bulletin board. Schedules from local yoga and dance studios are pinned over restaurant takeout cards. There's only one photo—of Caitlin and a young man. I pull it down and examine it.

It's the younger brother, Trevor—I see a family resemblance.

He's my ace in the hole. I have a guy watching the twenty-year-old kid who is an art student at the same university. No way my little hacker is going to try any funny business when I hold her brother's balls in a vise.

She'll return our money—steal it from someone else or do whatever she needs to do—and I'll consider letting both of them live.

Normally that wouldn't be Tacone policy, but she's a chick.

And a hot one at that.

Plus, I don't hurt women.

I look through her closet, smiling when I find the clothes I half expected or hoped to find. The vibe I got was right. She has kinky shit—Fishnets. Bootie shorts. Ripped sheer tops. Stripper gear, only she's not a stripper.

I fucking *knew* this girl was freaky.

I swear I could tell it from the photo. The computer geek thing just doesn't sit on her, despite the big black glasses and sloppy clothes. Something about her just screams sex. Maybe it's the candy-colored lip gloss on that wide-mouthed pout. Or the way she holds herself. She just *fucking embodies* carnal pleasure.

And that's why I've been looking forward to this meeting all week.

I glance at the clock. Almost showtime. I throw the clothes tossed over the easy chair onto the floor and make myself at home to wait.

I don't even bother taking out a gun to rest on my thigh like I might with a dude.

She'll be scared enough to find me in her apartment.

And I shouldn't let that give me a hard-on, but it does.

But even with my research and my own conjectures, I'm still unprepared for the hot sexy mess of a hacker who blows in.

She enters her apartment with earbuds in her ears, apparently still jamming out to her workout playlist. She's in a pair of yoga pants and puffy jacket, which she instantly strips to dump on the floor. Underneath, she's wearing a crop top that shows off a perfectly toned midriff below a pair of perky tits. Her dark hair is piled on top of her head in a thick, messy bun and she's wearing that bright lip gloss that makes me think about how that mouth would look around my dick.

She doesn't notice me as she comes in. She doesn't notice much of anything. She appears to be lost in thought as she walks straight to the kitchen, pours herself a bowl of Golden Grahams cereal and milk and starts eating standing up.

Only then does she turn and spot me.

The cereal bowl clatters to the floor as her scream pierces the air. Milk splatters fly everywhere.

Her wide eyes lock on mine, that pretty mouth opens.

But she recovers way faster than I expect. Just one short scream and she goes silent.

"Hello, Caitlin."

"Oh." Her palm travels down her toned belly, wiping at the milk splatters, then she dries it on her ass. And a very fine ass it is.

"The Tacones sent you?" She sounds breathless. Good. She was expecting me.

"I sent myself."

"Mr. Tacone, then."

And that's when I realize my usual intimidation schtick is a total and complete fail.

Because little miss hacker slowly slides her hand between her legs, holding my gaze while she curls her fingers there, touching herself like she's watching porn.

Or rather, like she's the porn star and she knows she owns me with that simple move.

∽

## *Caitlin*

"WHAT THE *FUCK* ARE YOU DOING?" my hitman demands. He has that decidedly urban, definitely dangerous way of saying *fuck*. When a college boy says *fuck,* it means nothing. The way this guy says it hits me square in the chest. It's an assault all in itself.

He's way more beautiful than I expected. Wickedly, darkly handsome, which seems unfair, since he's also a multi-millionaire.

*And a killer,* I remind myself as I seek my clit through my yoga pants. It is a manipulation. I'm trying to throw him off guard with my crazy. But it's also for me. Sex pulls me back to my body and I have to think now. I can't dissociate when my life is on the line here.

So I move my fingers slowly between my legs, rolling my clitoral hood piercing while I force myself to breathe and stare into the dark brown eyes of Chicago's Most Dangerous.

I always knew it would come to this. Me digging my own grave while a guy in an Italian suit holds a gun to my head. Only he doesn't even bother with a gun. It's like he knows, even sitting down without a visible weapon, I'm at his mercy.

I rub my clit harder, pushing the piercing against it for added friction, as my mouth goes slack and my nipples get hard, all the while watching the man in my apartment, looking for the opportunity to get away or kill him first. He raises his brows, and I realize he's waiting for an answer to his question.

I shrug like it's perfectly normal to finger yourself when you find a mafia hitman in your apartment. "If I'm gonna die, I'm at least going to make it feel good. You know, make it my fantasy, not yours," I tell him. I try to make it sound like I'm not scared at all.

And that's partly true. Life will fuck you hard in the ass, so you might as well find a way to enjoy it. That's been my mantra since the day my dad disappeared. Since the night social services showed up and took my brother and me away to separate foster homes.

"Yeah?" The Tacone—I don't know which of the five brothers he is because he hasn't told me—slowly unfolds his long legs from my easy chair and rises. He's tall and stocky—over six feet, with broad shoulders. Despite the size and hulk, he saunters toward me with an effortless, casual grace. And he's not pissed off by my masturbation. Judging by the bulge in his pants, he's enjoying my show. Which means sex is a place I can find leverage with him.

I'm definitely not above using the only things I have—my sexuality and lack of sanity—to fight back in an unwinnable situation.

He pulls two zip ties from his jacket pocket, a grin playing at the corners of his mouth. "So what *is* your fantasy, little hacker?" He catches my wrists and pins them together in front, then wraps a zip tie around them.

And with that simple act—his taking control of my body—some more of my sanity slips, because now he's got kinky Caitlin under his thumb.

The zip tie hurts, so I twist my wrists against the hard plastic, letting it dig into my skin, keep me in my body.

I return my bound hands to my pulsing clit and continue a slow rub. Mr. Tacone watches.

Then he feeds right into my fantasy and pinches one of my nipples through my shirt and sports bra. He holds it tight and twists. "I asked you a question, Caitlin. I expect an answer." His voice is low and smoky. It curls between my legs, creating shivers of pleasure tremoring through my body.

*Don't get lost in lust,* I warn myself. It's a delicate line. I use sex to stay in my body, but I can just as easily lose myself there, as well. And I didn't expect my hitman to be quite so… appealing. I'm losing the sliver of leverage I imagined I had.

My eyelids flutter. If I were wearing panties, I would've soaked them. As it is, I'm bare under my yoga pants so there's probably a wet spot.

Tacone tosses me easily over his shoulder and carries me the few steps it takes to get to my bed, where he throws me down and fastens another zip tie around my ankles. When I roll to my side, he slaps my ass.

"What's the fantasy, little thief?"

I wriggle my ass around on the bed. "Some more of that," I purr. It's meant to goad him.

Not because I'm dripping for this. Not because I'm fuck-nut crazy.

Not because the worse things get for me, the more I look to pain and sex as a frame I can deal with.

Shockingly, my hitman takes the bait. He holds my hips still with one hand and claps the other one down on my ass a couple times. *Hard.* He's not screwing around. "That right?"

I roll to my belly, reaching my bound wrists above my head to get there. Twerk my ass for more.

Major qualms peak, though, when he unbuckles his belt and pulls it from the loops.

This guy is for real. This isn't one of the doms I've scened with to get my fix. He came here to hurt me—probably kill me. So I should be terrified. And I am. But... it also makes this one hundred times hotter than some consensual, pre-negotiated scene. Because the danger is real. The risk is considerably higher.

A therapist could have a field day with this.

He winds the buckle end of the belt around his hand in a quick, efficient manner. And then it's on. The first strike lands right across the middle of my ass. Pain lights up my pleasure centers.

*Yes!*

I lift my butt for more. He leathers the hell out of my ass, striking the lower half of my buttocks over and over again until I'm breathless and hot and heady with endorphin release.

"Like that?" he says after more than two dozen stripes.

I roll onto my back and bring my hands between my legs again.

"Did I say you could fucking touch yourself?" He grabs my bound wrists and pries them away.

Holy shit. Either this guy is just a total natural at playing dominant asshole or he's part of the kink scene, same as me.

"Please," I whimper, because why not try? One more orgasm is my dying request.

The kink gods smile on me, because he holds my

wrists prisoner with one hand and brings the thumb of his other hand to my clit and rubs, firm and quick.

Surprise flares in his eyes when he discovers my piercing but he quickly learns to work it like a pro.

My eyes roll back in my head. I gasp and hold my breath. I go off almost immediately, bending and straightening my bound legs like a frog, my internal muscles squeezing and clenching around nothing.

Tacone mutters something in Italian—it sounds like a curse, and then he unzips his slacks and pulls out his cock. I experience a moment of cold fear at being raped before the crazy takes back over, and I own the scene again.

When he fists his erection and strokes from base to tip, I scooch around on the bed to bring my face toward his crotch. He stops me before my mouth reaches his cock, catching the bun on the top of my head and pulling my hair taut. "Not sure I trust you to put your mouth on my cock, doll," he tells me.

I open my lips, offering a clear invitation.

He shakes his head but brings his cock to my mouth. "I feel even one tooth and this will be the last fucking cock you ever see. *Capiche*?"

Crazy Caitlin jots a tally mark in my column. There's always power in giving head, even bound and at his mercy.

"Yes, sir," I say automatically, BDSM protocol drilled into me.

Still gripping my hair, he plunges his cock into my mouth and down my throat. "Yes, Mr. Tacone," he corrects.

"Yes, Mr. Tacone," I agree when he pulls my mouth back off his cock.

He shoves back in. "Make it good, little hacker. One hundred and fifty thousand dollars good."

A spike of fear shoots through me at the reminder of how much I stole from them, but crazy Caitlin steps forward again. Might as well enjoy the last cock I'm going to see. It's no hardship, either, because my body's still glorying in the rush of endorphins. My ass still smarts and throbs from a delicious whipping and I just orgasmed hard.

"Good girl," he praises and I lose myself, eyes closed, head bobbing, tongue swirling with enthusiasm.

I make it as good as I know how. I've been told I give good head. This could be the blowjob that saves my life.

∽

*Paolo*

This can't be for real.

Thirty minutes into my visit and she's sucking my cock like her life depends on it.

Okay, she probably *does* believe her life depends on it. A better man would feel bad about shoving his cock in the mouth of a girl he has tied up on her bed, but I don't.

She fucking offered. Her freak flag is flying high.

And yeah, I definitely think it's still possible she'll try to bite the whole thing off. Girl is a nut-job.

But it feels so.

Damn.

Good.

I choke her every time I shove it deep down her throat.

I watch her eyes tear up as she struggles to breathe, but she keeps going right back to her enthusiastic sucking.

I want it to last forever. I wonder how long she can go? Twenty minutes? Half hour? She definitely has mad skills. But then she moans around my cock, like she's turned on giving me head, and my balls tighten up. Fuck it. I'll let her off easy this time since she's being so good.

I burrow my fingers in her hair, flicking off the scrunchy that holds it in a bun and letting the dark mess fall free. Her hair is long and thick.

Wild, like her.

I wrap my fist around it and hold her head immobile as I fuck her face faster, disrespecting the hell out of her without even an ounce of regret.

"I'm coming, doll. You gonna swallow like a good girl?"

Her blue eyes meet mine and she nods and makes a sound.

I come, pulling her hair even tighter.

She swallows and swallows. Works her tongue around my dick to clean me off.

And then intimidation goes out the window. I stroke her cheek. Her skin is soft and smooth. She's pale-complexioned, with a dusting of the cutest freckles across her nose. The glasses sit askew on her face.

I massage her scalp, trying to rub away the sting from all the hair-pulling, still dipping my cock in and out of her mouth.

I pull out and run my thumb over her generous mouth. I have the urge to kiss those glossy lips, but I resist it.

Post-blowjob gratitude comes on hard—heh—and I study Caitlin, fascinated by everything I see.

This woman is a fucking unicorn. The kind who shouldn't exist.

What kind of genius hacker also has a hot-as-fuck body and goads a guy into freaky sex when she should be shaking in her boots?

This one, apparently.

And I might be in love.

If I believed in love, that is.

But seriously. She's everything I got from her photo and more, and I want to know every last thing about her. I want to turn her inside out, break her. Build her up. Break her again.

Worship her.

Because right now, I'm feeling grateful and I want to taste that pussy of hers.

I yank her leggings all the way down to the zip ties at her ankles, then lift her ankles high in the air to get a look at the damage I did on her ass. Not too bad. Red and puffy welts. I'd feel bad but it seemed like she enjoyed every second of it.

I rub my palm over the welts I left, squeezing her muscular buns, slapping them. Now that I've gotten aggressive with her, I fucking love how it feels. I've never laid a hand on a woman before, but I could spank this girl all night.

"How's your ass?" I ask, just to be completely sure I'm reading her right.

She blinks up at me. The crazed glassy look is gone from those blue eyes now. I see intelligence and a trace of uncertainty in her gaze. "I could've taken more." It doesn't come out as a challenge. Not like she's bragging or daring me to give her more. Instead it sounds like an admission she's not sure she should make. She's being honest. Like I'm her sex partner and we're going to do this again.

Fuck. I adjust my cock. I just came, but I'm already getting hard again.

I flick my brows. "Noted." I spank her several more times, much harder than before.

She yelps, her ass jerking in the air. I spank over her pussy and my palm comes away wet.

I lower her ass to the bed and spread her knees wide.

She gasps, her lips forming a pretty "O", her glazed eyes wide and startled.

Her pussy's waxed bare, which both pleases and infuriates me at the same time. Like, who in the fuck is she keeping it bare for?

I suddenly want to kill every motherfucker who's been here before me.

And everyone who will be here after me.

*Don't let there be any after you,* the possessive voice in my head growls.

Which is stupid, because I'm not keeping her. I came to get my money back, that's all. Relationships are for pussies.

I shove her top and sports bra up over her tits and take a moment to drink in the sight. Her perky breasts are forced down by the tight band of the sports bra, which makes them jut out, straining for freedom. Her nipples are peach-tipped, skin is pale. She's like Snow White with almost black hair and pale white skin. The blue eyes bring a shock of color to the palette.

She shivers under my gaze, which produces a feral smile on my lips. Locking eyes with her, I slowly lower my head between her legs. I lick into her, my tongue parting her labia and tracing around the inside.

Her knees jerk and slam closed around my ears. I push them back open, holding her inner thighs with a bruising grip and flick my tongue over her clit. She has a pierced hood, which is hot as hell. This girl is as kinky as they come.

"Oh...oh! Ohmygod. So good," she moans.

I enjoy her enthusiastic appreciation and take it up a notch. I lap her juices, working faster, then rim her anus and make her squeal. Her inner thighs tremble against my shoulders. Her belly flutters as she gasps and lets out shuddering exhales.

"My God. Mr. Tacone... big man, big bossman."

I chuckle against her soft flesh at the stream of words coming from her lips.

She's adorable.

She writhes beneath me and I lash her clit and piercing in quick flicks as I screw one finger inside her.

I bring my thumb to her anus and massage a circle around it. "Here's what's going to happen. I'm going to suck your little clitty and count to four. And you're gonna come all over my face by the time I'm done counting. *Capiche*?"

She likes it. She nods quickly, her pupils so big in her eyes, they look black.

"Good girl. Here we go." I lower my head and flick her

clit a few more times, then suction my lips over it. The piercing helps keep the hood back and makes it easier to suck.

She comes on the count of two.

Obedient, responsive, crazy little thing.

I *am* in love.

I want to keep her.

Should I keep her?

Nah. It would get old quickly. And she's clearly a nutjob. Plus, she has a life. Graduate studies. A career.

She may have fucked the Tacones, but I'm not willing to take all that from her.

She just needs to make things right and then I'll let her go.

No harm, no foul.

When her orgasm abates, I lick her some more, nipping one of her lips. Then I pull her pants up, unable to resist a few more swipes over her clit after I do.

"Are you going to kill me?" she croaks.

Back to business.

"We'll see," I tell her, because I'm a dick. I'm a dick and I don't mind her scared. Especially now that I know it turns her on as much as it does me.

## CHAPTER 2

*C*aitlin

Mr. Tacone saunters into my kitchen and picks up the water bottle I left on the counter. When he brings it back to me to sip, my confusion is complete.

As much as I want to, I can't believe I just softened this guy up by sucking his dick. I mean, maybe a little, but he's still here to kill me.

Maybe he's like the cat who likes to play with his victims first. Well, that's good. More time for me to work out how to get myself out of this pickle. Plus, I love the way he plays. He's better than any of the wanna-be doms at the local dungeon. Better-looking. Bossier. Handy with a belt.

He leaves me with the water bottle and walks around my apartment, picking things up and examining them. He opens my satchel—the one I always carry with me and pulls everything out. My laptop, my wallet, the workout clothes I changed out of after my shower at the rec center. He looks at the wet, sweaty clothes, then over at me, his eyes running over my outfit.

"I live in yoga pants," I explain. "These are clean, or they were, before you made me leak all over them."

His lips twitch. He continues his perusal of my things, scrolling through all the messages on my phone, opening the laptop and clicking buttons.

Finally, he pulls the armchair around to face me on the bed and sits down.

"So, Caitlin."

"Yes, sir." I'm lying on my side, ankles and wrists bound, my ass still pulsing with heat from his whipping and the taste of his cum still in my mouth. I definitely feel submissive, even as I look for some kind of escape.

He crosses his long legs and loosens his tie. I wonder if he dressed up for me or if this is what he always wears when he shows up to kill someone. Like it's the mafia work uniform or something.

"Of all the casinos in Vegas, you picked ours. It feels a little personal, doll. Was it?"

I should've expected this question and had an answer, but for some reason, it takes me by surprise. I can't hide the truth from my expression or make an answer come quickly enough to sound legit.

"No." My voice has a warble to it.

He tips his head to the side. "There are consequences for lying to me." The threat rolls off his tongue easily. Silkily, even. I swear, the doms at the dungeon should take lessons from this guy.

"So it *was* personal. You live in Chicago—our city. You have a beef with one of us?" He watches my expression, which I try very hard to keep blank. "Which one? My father? You're a little young for that."

His father—Don Tacone—is in jail. Has been for the last ten years or so. I know that much from my research. The truth is, I don't know which Tacone did it or gave the order. I just know they're responsible.

I shake my head. "No beef. I just knew of your family from living here and how you'd expanded into the casino business in Vegas."

He doesn't move, just watches me, and I know he knows it's bullshit. Interesting that he doesn't follow through on the threat of consequences.

It actually frightens me more. Another whipping I could take. A little torture.

Not knowing what he's thinking chills me to the core.

"I have to pee." It's not a lie. But I also desperately need to get away from his close scrutiny.

He remains still, studying me for a moment longer, then stands up from the chair. Without a word, he scoops me into his arms, then tosses me into the air to shift me into the ignominious sack of potatoes position over his shoulder. And of course, his hand slaps down on my ass.

It does all kinds of exciting things to my body.

I channel the tingles, the kick of lust at being so easily manhandled by such a large, capable, dangerous man into figuring a way out of this. I could grab a razor from the shower to use on him.

But I know that's stupid. A man with big ham hands like him could fight me off with his little finger, even if I did have a sharp blade. Escape would be a better option. I just need to get my ankles free to run.

Are there scissors in the bathroom? I look around desperately when he puts me down, but I already know there's nothing there. My apartment may be messy, but I'm the type who knows exactly where everything is in the mess.

No scissors in the bathroom. Maybe nail clippers.

My hitman tucks his thumbs in the waistband of my yoga pants and drags them down my thighs. After what he's already done, it shouldn't make me blush, but it does. There's something even more intimate about peeing on a toilet in front of someone than sucking his cock.

He lowers me to sit on the toilet and stands right over me, arms crossed.

Okay, getting the nail clippers out of the drawer may not be possible with this level of supervision.

Fuck!

I stare up at him for a moment. My nipples are hard.

"I thought you had to pee." His voice is a deep, authoritative rumble.

"It's hard when you're staring at me! Can I have a little privacy, please?"

"No."

Damn. I look away, finding a spot on the floor to concentrate on, because it wasn't a lie. I can't seem to break the seal. I inhale slowly. Hold my breath. Exhale.

Mr. Tacone doesn't move. I draw back my bound wrists and bop him on the leg. "You're enjoying this a little too much, don't you think?"

I see that glimmer of a smile. "Definitely."

I huff, but the exchange normalized things enough for me to pee. My body relaxes and I'm able to let it out.

I look up at him with a challenge. "Could you hand me some toilet paper? I can't reach." I twist and jerk my arms and feign pathetic.

I don't know why I'm trying to annoy him— just to take a little power back, I guess, but he seems far more amused than annoyed. He rolls up a ball of toilet paper and presses it into my bound hands.

It's freaking hard to wipe and takes me a few tries, but I manage and stand up.

He pulls up my pants and I fall into him, my bound hands grabbing a fistful of his crisp shirt as he bands one strong arm around me. He smells clean and masculine. I would've figured him for the heavy cologne type, but all I detect is the light scent of soap and the smell of his skin.

He heaves me easily over his shoulder again. "All right, Caitlin. Back to the bed for you. We have time to kill before I can move you. Time enough for you to spill all your secrets." He dumps me back on the bed.

"Where are you moving me to?" I ask quickly, both to distract him from his questions and because, yeah. I need to know where my final resting place will be, if that's what he's planning.

"I ask the questions, little hacker. Why my casino?"

Goosebumps rise on my arms. I give a one shouldered shrug, because I'm lying on the other one. "I'd heard of it."

He narrows his eyes. "You're a smart girl, Caitlin— obviously. You've been stealing from us for years and you only just now got caught. It was a clever setup, too. Took skill and a lot of thought to complete. There's no way I believe you'd pick the one casino in Vegas run by Sicilians for your scam unless you had a good reason. If you wanted any casino to skim from, there are at least a hundred better choices."

I try to look away from his gaze, but find it impossible. Instead, my stupid face heats.

He looms over me and grips my jaw, lowering his face to mine. He really is handsome. Dark, curling lashes, chocolate brown eyes. No smile lines. This guy takes shit seriously. "So don't fucking lie to me. I wanna know what was going through that beautiful head of yours when you picked the Bellissimo."

I'm not going to tell him.

At least I don't plan to.

But he's gained such control of my body that my mind seems to follow. Or maybe I just want him to know they deserved it. If I'm going to die for this, I can at least make my point before I do.

"You killed my father," I whisper.

∾

*Paolo*

I RELEASE my hold on her face and draw back, surprised. "Oh yeah?"

It's possible. I've killed a lot of men. None who didn't deserve everything they got. I think back to what I read in her file about her father's death. It certainly hadn't been enough information to ring a bell with me, if there is a bell to ring.

"Me, personally, or someone in the organization?"

She looks away. She's been trying to look away for a while now, but I had her locked into an uncomfortable stare-down. "I'm not sure who actually pulled the trigger."

"But he was shot?"

She doesn't answer.

"You don't know for sure."

Now she lifts her eyes again. She wants answers. That's why she let me find her. It makes perfect sense. Smart girl like her wouldn't leave me any path to her door, but she did. Course she is a bit of a trainwreck. And she has that penchant for punishment.

But no, some part of her wanted me to show up here and give her answers about her father's death. I've seen this kind of obsession before. It's damn hard when there's no body. You never fully put the person to rest.

"He disappeared and you think we had something to do with it."

Again, she lifts her gaze. Damn beautiful gaze, too. Those blue eyes are striking as hell. She nods.

Damn. This girl is getting under my skin. I'm already regretting shoving my cock in her mouth.

But no. She offered—I didn't force.

And I gave her pleasure afterward. Still have the taste of her on my tongue.

I don't show any of the sympathy she inspires in me. I just blink down at her with an authoritative, disapproving gaze.

But I almost wish I had something to tell her. Give her

that closure she desires. But that's stupid. Even if I knew what happened to her dad, I wouldn't admit it. It's not like I can drive her out and show her a burial site so she can leave flowers. We'd be talking about a capital offense. Murder One. Doesn't matter how much I want to help her, it's not something I would admit to. Not unless I planned on killing her afterward.

"What makes you think we were involved in his disappearance?"

She purses her lips and shifts her gaze to a point on the wall. "He was working for you. The police asked all about his dealings with the Tacones when he disappeared. They pretty much inferred you did it but they couldn't prove it."

I seriously don't remember any guy named West working for us. We keep things tight. Sicilians only. No outsiders. I make a doubtful sound. "Cops think we committed hundreds of crimes we had no part in."

Her eyes narrow.

"Name was West?"

"Lake West."

"Lake." That name does jog something. It's a memorable name—strange I didn't notice it when I was reading her file. But I hadn't been looking for a connection. I seem to recall a lowlife thief by that name. Douchey type. Skinny white guy with ripped faded blue jeans and facial hair that wasn't all the way filled in.

Well, shit. Maybe we did kill him.

"Thief like you?" I almost regret the question, because her face flushes a deep shade of pink and her jaw sets tight. But I already started this line of questioning, might as well make my point. "Yeah? Stealing from the Tacones never ends well, doll."

I see that flash of vulnerability on her face. Grief and fear mingled with defiance. And then, just like that, her eyes go dull.

Like she checked out and no one's home.

I push back the sympathy I feel for her. It's because of what she already showed me. Her freaky side. The fact that she sucked my cock. Rolled around on that bed while I whipped her ass.

And fuck if I didn't enjoy hurting her that way.

I always knew I had a sadistic streak, I just never let myself indulge. Our dad might have taught us to rule this city with brutal violence and intimidation, but he also taught us to respect women. He never took a mistress or cheated on our mother. Always treated her like she was a goddess.

And me? I'm not the dates and dancing type. I'm the fuck 'em hard and kick them out before morning type, so relationships have never been my thing.

Looking down at this wildfire of a woman beneath me —and she is all woman, despite her college student status —I wonder if maybe I just hadn't found the right kind of woman before. I didn't know women like Caitlin existed.

Women who like it as hard and rough as I like to give. Who don't get offended or cry because I'm an inconsiderate *stronzo* who will never say he cares. She *enjoyed* being hurt by me.

*Cristo*, it gets my dick hard again thinking about whipping that girl's ass. How she moaned and rubbed herself while I did it. Told me she could've taken more.

I walk away from her now, because that bright flame of hers burned out the moment I called her on her shit.

The moment I pointed out there are no innocent victims here. Her daddy probably stole from us and got what he deserved. And the same is going to happen to her, minus the killing part.

She's going to pay every red cent back before I let her walk away from this with the threat that'll keep her scared of me for the rest of her life.

Funny how I don't feel much satisfaction in that at the moment.

Crazy girls fuck with your head.

That's the only explanation I can come up with for how I'm feeling right now.

## CHAPTER 3

*Caitlin*

Sometimes it's hard for me to distinguish fear from excitement. I have an intelligent, rational mind, but as soon as it lands on something that scares me, I leave my body. And the way I come back is through sex and pain.

So getting bound, whipped and face-fucked by the mafia kingpin who showed up to kill me? Didn't scare me.

Talking about my dad's death shut me down, though.

And when my hitman packs up my electronic equipment, throws me over his shoulder and carries me out of the apartment, real fear sets in.

"Mr. Tacone?" I mumble, swinging over his wide shoulder. I have a close-up view of his ass, and it's quite impressive, I have to say. He's definitely an Italian Stallion, this one.

Who knew?

I might have played my cards differently if I'd known skimming over a hundred thousand dollars would trigger a hitman in such a handsome, dominant package.

He slaps my ass. "Not a sound, little hacker. Do you want me to gag you?"

Ugh. Why does that turn me on? He scrambles my brain when he says things like that. I need to figure out how to escape instead of getting wet every time he says something bossy.

"No, sir," I mutter.

"Good girl."

There's no elevator in my building, but he's not even winded after carrying me down four flights of stairs and out into the parking lot. I look around, but there's no one to hear me scream. He waited until the middle of the night to kidnap me.

I should've screamed back in the building. One of my neighbors might have come out or called the cops. Why didn't I?

I swear sometimes I don't have any sense. For a girl who got a 1410 on her SATs, I'm pretty stupid.

Or I have a deathwish.

That has a ring of truth in it. Which is why I targeted the Tacones in the first place. That, and for revenge.

They deserve to pay for what they did.

The Tacone guy—still don't know which one he is—pops the trunk of his Porsche and cold washes through me.

Now I'm going to die. I'm definitely going to die.

I try to swing off his shoulder, even though with my ankles zip tied together I wouldn't make it one step away. He slaps my ass but he's careful putting me in the trunk.

Like he's laying down a sleeping baby or something.

He stares down at me for a moment, his expression inscrutable.

I'm shaking all over. "Please," I beg. "I don't want to die."

He shrugs off his jacket and lays it over me, carefully tucking the edges around my body to keep it on.

*Huh.*

Maybe I'm not going to die. Yet. What kind of hitman tucks his jacket around his victim to make sure she doesn't get too cold?

"Please, Mr. Tacone."

The trunk slams closed and I choke back a sob.

Shit! Fuck a duck. This is bad. Very bad.

My breath comes in little pants as the car roars to life and pulls away from the curb.

I'm so dead I'm so dead I'm so dead.

I don't want to die.

That realization strikes me a little too late.

Too bad I continuously engage in risky behavior.

"I don't want to die!" I scream, as if that might somehow convince the hitman to let me live. "Mr. Tacone!" I shriek. "Let me out of here." I shriek until I'm hoarse, but of course it does no good. I can't reach the emergency latch to open the trunk, and can't get enough power with my ankles bound to kick out the lights.

Eventually the car rolls to a stop and the engine shuts off.

Now is when I should scream, but my throat is sore and dry and I've exhausted myself.

The trunk opens and the Tacone brother stares down at

me. "Not a fan of the screaming," he says, pinning me with a look.

That's all he says.

Strangely, that's all he needs to say. It's like we both know I won't do it again. He threatened a gag earlier, and I don't want to make him follow through on that threat.

Also because he's that dominant and something in me likes to submit.

Keeping his jacket wrapped around my shoulders, he hauls me up over his shoulder again and carries me into what seems to be a single-family dwelling in the suburbs.

Well, okay. He's probably not planning to kill me here.

Or it seems unlikely. Too much blood.

And noise.

If he'd pulled me out of the trunk in some remote wooded location I would've been sure it was time to dig my grave. But this looks like it could be his house.

*Huh.*

He carries me inside. I lift my head and attempt to look around. It's a beautiful modern home with luxurious furnishings. It smells like him— earthy male and leather. He carries me into what must be his bedroom and drops me on the king-sized bed. The comforter is an iridescent gun-metal grey. "Don't move," he says and walks out of the room.

Yeah, right. I'm not that stupid. I quickly scan the room and my eyes land on a pair of nail clippers on the bedside table.

*Bingo!*

I lunge for them, army crawling with my elbows across the bed and snatching them up. One snip and the ankle ties are free. I don't waste time with the wrist ties, I just launch off the bed, palming the clippers as I run for the front door.

I'm almost there when something thin and soft wraps around my throat and jerks me back.

I drag in a desperate gasp, my fingers flying to the material at my throat.

His tie.

He's choking me with his tie.

Except he's not. He alternates cutting off my air flow and letting me breathe.

The man knows exactly what he's doing.

He's probably killed dozens of people this way while he forces their final confessions out of them. Did my father die this way?

"I thought I told you not to move." His voice is even. Deep. Seductive, but I don't think that's what he's aiming for.

I've never been into breathplay—it seems too risky to me—but I pretend this is sex, a scene. Something that could be ended with a simple utterance of my safeword. And just by flipping the scenario into sex-land—same as I did at my place earlier—my fear ebbs away. The blank panic fades. My body comes alive.

I let my head fall back on his shoulder and rub my bound hands between my legs.

His chuckle is soft. His lips are right at my ear.

"You like to get choked out while you're getting it hard, Caitlin?"

*Oh gawd.* The man picks up what I'm putting down without even missing a beat.

"Maybe," I admit. But there's no maybe about it. I'm already wet. "Have you practiced breathplay?"

And the tactic totally works, because he forgets about pulling the tie taut around my neck, instead sliding one hand down my belly and into my pants. When he slowly swipes one finger over my slit, I'm shockingly slick and wet.

"I've choked a few people, yeah. You wanna try?"

I don't miss noticing that he's asking. It seems incongruent with everything else he's done, and I take it as a good sign. Maybe he's one of those guys who's fine with killing a woman but not with raping her.

It sort of fits the mafia profile—at least the one portrayed in movies and television. They may be dangerous and operate outside the law but there's still a code they live by. They just honor their own rules.

Maybe his rule is not to force himself on a woman. Or maybe it's just his pride. I sort of doubt he would ever have to force. Not with those looks and the money and power behind them. Women probably throw their panties at him on a daily basis.

Which is precisely what I'm going to do.

"Yes, big man."

He sinks one of his fingers into my channel. "Big man, huh? Babygirl, this is the strangest direction a shakedown has ever gone for me, you know that?"

I go still. "This is a shakedown?"

Not a murder. He would've said *hit* if it was supposed to be a hit, right?

With his hand still down my pants, he uses the tie around my neck to swivel me around and march me back toward the bedroom. "It's whatever I want it to be. Right now, it's me bending you over that bed and fucking you hard from behind with this tie wrapped tight around your throat. *Capiche?*"

I moan. I don't even know if he means this as dirty talk, but to me it works like magic. "I *capiche*," I say.

He snorts because I'm sure that's not how you say it. Whatever. When we reach the bed, he pushes my torso down over the side of it and screws a second finger into me. I tuck my forearms under my chest and rock my hips to get him deeper. He bites my shoulder as he removes his fingers and I gasp. With quick, deft movements, he rids me of my yoga pants. I hear the tear of foil and I'm instantly grateful he's responsible, because I hadn't even thought about protection. At least I'm on the pill.

And the fact that he's using a condom... does that mean he's not killing me? Or is it just to protect him from anything I might be carrying?

Probably the latter. That thought tanks my initial elation.

The tie around my neck had gone loose but he cinches it again, sliding it up right beneath my chin so when he pulls on it, he lifts my head and bows my back.

"Aw, that's pretty, doll. Really fucking pretty."

I suddenly feel it. I picture how I must look to him; tied up, choked and ready to be fucked and it's definitely hot.

He shoves into me from behind. It's rough and forceful and just how I like it. My body was ready for him, even though he's big. He thrusts in deep, easing out and bumping my ass when he slams back in.

I clench my pussy around his large cock and he jerks, shoving in harder. "Damn, you feel good, *bella*. You practice keeping that pussy so tight?"

"Yes," I admit. Aren't we all supposed to be doing our kegels?

He mutters something that sounds like, "*Cazzo*." Must be an Italian curse.

I love the way he fucks me hard, like it's punishment, like I'm meant to feel where he's been for days. My ass is still sore from the whipping and each time he slams in, his loins slap against it, renewing the sensation, winding my crank tighter and tighter.

He tightens the silk tie around my neck, cutting off my air flow. The lack of oxygen, or maybe the fear and desperation that come with being choked bring me right to the precipice of orgasm, but he releases it before I get there.

I let out a frustrated moan.

When he pulls out, I flip my hair over my shoulder to turn and glare at him.

He smirks. "You don't deserve to have me come in your pussy. You've been a bad girl." He slaps my butt. "You're going to take it in the ass."

I shiver. I may be into pain, but anal's not my thing. It's too personal. Too intimate. "Lube!" I cry out defensively. "You can use anything—olive oil, coconut oil. Whatever you have. Please."

He snorts again. "I ought to shred your ass with no lube," he says, but he gets up and opens a dresser drawer, producing a bottle of lubricant.

Thank God.

"Climb up on the bed," he orders, as if I have full use of my hands. I pull my knees up onto the bed and he helps situate me in the middle of it. "Ass in the air, troublemaker." He slaps my butt to punctuate the command.

If I stopped for even a moment to consider how strange and crazy it is that I turned my shakedown into a BDSM extravaganza, I would laugh until I cried. But I'm too lost in the moment. Too turned on, too surrendered in submissive mode. The guy could probably do anything to me right now and I'd let him.

And that's the danger of my quirks.

*Risky behavior,* is what the school counselor told the social worker back in high school when I filed for emancipation.

I don't care. In this moment, it feels good.

My would-be hitman shoves my upper body down on the mattress and dribbles an ample amount of lube over my crack.

Again, thank God.

With one side of my face pressed to the bedcovers, I watch the man behind me unbutton his dress shirt and tug it off. *Dayum.* What I see makes my pussy clench in anticipation. He's not what I expected. I mean, yes, he's a big burly bear of a man with wide, muscled shoulders and ample chest hair curling above his undershirt. But there's no flashy gold chain or rings on his fingers. The suit is obviously expensive but very tasteful.

He's classy.

That's the part that surprises me. This isn't the street thug mafia man from the movies.

Scratch that. I rode here in the trunk of his car and he's

about to buttfuck me for trying to escape. Except it doesn't feel that way. It feels like two people engaged in consensual nonconsent. An extended scene at the local BDSM club.

"All right, little girl. You ready to have your ass fucked?"

"Um…"

Is he waiting for a green light? After he told me I deserved to have my ass shredded by him? He rubs my pussy, playing with my clit until my knees slide wider on the bed.

"You look ready, *bella.*" He pressed the tip of his cock against my anus.

Even though I know the trick is to relax, I tighten.

He waits.

When the tight ring of muscles finally relaxes, he pushes forward.

I gasp and tighten again.

"Lie flat, little hacker, it will loosen things up."

It will? Okay. I slide my knees back until I'm on my belly. He pushes my cheeks wide and dribbles more lube over my anus. Then he resumes entry. He's right. This time it's not as tight. He gets in and it stretches, but it's not horrible. I breathe through it, my eyes squeezed closed. When he's finally seated, he waits.

I forgot about the tie around my neck, but he didn't. He picks it up and pulls it tight. My back bows up and I lean on my elbows to take the pressure off, but my hitman has started rocking in and out of my ass. Just a tiny movement, but it feels…

Really good.

Yeah, really freaking good.

I start making sounds. Moans of discomfort and pleasure mingled together.

He pumps a little harder—increases the range of his strokes. Tightens the leash around my neck.

"Ow, please," I whimper, but I don't want him to stop.

"Please, what, little hacker? Please fuck me harder?"

My pussy is swollen, sopping. Wanting something inside it, but he's abusing my ass. I've never felt so used, so punished, so submissive in my life.

It's a heady sensation. The endorphins course through my bloodstream. I'm on the edge of an orgasm.

"Please," I moan again.

"Please you need to come?"

"Yes!"

He tightens the pressure around my throat at the same time he increases the speed of his pumps.

I try to beg some more, but the sound is choked off with my breath. I want to touch my pussy, shove my fingers in it, give it something to clamp down on, but I can't move. I'm held prisoner by the band around my neck and the cock in my ass.

My orgasm rips through me. I tighten around his cock and he curses and releases the tie.

I suck in breath as I tumble face forward into the mattress, face forward into release. He holds me down by my nape and fucks my ass hard and fast while I float far, far away.

I hardly hear his shout when he comes. Don't even know what happened after that.

The next thing I know, he's put a new zip tie around

my ankles and removed the one on my wrists long enough to pull off my shirt and sports bra. And then he must've put a new zip tie around my wrists, but I missed when that happened, because I'm suddenly in a bathtub filling with warm water and he's standing over me, looking very stern as he strips out of his clothes.

"You move from this tub and I'll shove something even bigger than my cock up your ass and it will stay there until you've returned my money. *Capiche*?"

I blink at him. What did he say? It didn't even make sense.

I can't return his money. The money is gone. Does he think I have it?

He steps into the adjacent shower and turns it on. "I'm watching you."

It's not funny, but I giggle. Just because he's sexy when he's stern, and I just hit subspace and am still riding my way back down.

I close my eyes and sink down into the warm, delicious water of the bath. I know I have problems. Huge, deadly ones. But just for this moment, I let myself forget. Surrender to the water and the will of my captor.

And aftermath of the best scene and sex of my life.

∼

*Paolo*

CAITLIN DOESN'T MOVE from the bath. She doesn't even

look around for a weapon, like she did in her bathroom. The girl is in outer space.

She's definitely cray-cray. Like way off from normal.

Not sure why I find her so damn appealing.

Hot mess crazy isn't my thing. I mean, I'd usually run away from that shit at the first sign.

But something about this little girl has already burrowed way under my skin. I feel strangely protective of her.

And her crazy thing doesn't make me uncomfortable. It amuses me. Like I've chuckled more tonight than I have in the last month.

I keep an eye on her through the foggy glass of the shower door. She looks beautiful with her head tipped back, her wide mouth curved in pleasure.

I want to give her far more.

Too bad that's not going to jive well with the demands I'm about to put on her. Which is the only reason I'm putting it off.

I can lay down the law tomorrow. Tonight it's late and she's gotta be falling asleep in that tub after what I put her through.

I shut off the water and grab a towel. She doesn't open her eyes when I step out and dry off. Not until I pull the drain plug on the tub and the water starts emptying. Then she only lifts her lids halfway and watches me.

It's damn sexy.

"It's not going to be so easy lifting me out of this tub," she observes and again, I'm tempted to smile.

"You gonna make it hard?"

"No." She sounds surprised, like she hadn't thought of resisting. "I just don't see how you're going to do it."

"Easy." I grip her forearms and lift her up enough to sit her on the side of the tub.

"Oh," she says, like she's embarrassed. "Yeah, I guess it was easy."

I wrap a towel around her body and dry her off, then scoop her into my arms to carry to the bed. I want to keep her naked, but I have to remind myself she's not mine. She may have initiated all the crazy shit we did tonight, but that doesn't mean I can spread those toned legs in the morning and pound out my morning wood.

And I definitely will if she sleeps naked. Probably wouldn't even wait until morning.

I put on a pair of boxer briefs and grab one of my t-shirts for her. I have to unclip the zip tie to put it on her. The skin of her wrists is getting raw and bruised, which I don't love, but I can't trust her enough to leave her unbound, either. I grab my tie and wrap it around her wrists a few times first, then use the zip tie over it, so she at least has some padding.

"Will you do that for my ankles too?" she asks innocently. Like she's asking for a glass of Coke from a waiter.

I shove her onto her back and lift her ankles in the air, taking the opportunity to slap her ass a few times.

She shrieks.

"These ankles?"

"Yes, please."

I can't help myself. Putting a little hurt on her is so fucking satisfying. I had no idea what a sadistic *stronzo* I was with a woman until now. I paddle her ass all over with my hand, the crack of flesh on flesh and her resulting gasps loud in the bedroom.

I give her extra spanks over her pussy, which protrudes enticingly through her legs. I don't stop until her ass is red and warm under my hand. Only then do I snip off the zip tie and use one of my socks under a fresh one to keep it from rubbing.

Her cornflower blue gaze is on my face the whole time. The blankness she displayed in the bathroom is gone. I see the keen intelligence now. "What are you going to do with me?" she asks.

"You're going to make reparations. And after you do, I might let you go. We'll see."

I know I didn't straight out tell her I'd set her free, but I meant the words to put her a little more at ease. Because I know she's been wondering if I'm going to off her. But she goes pale at my pronouncement, her face shuttering up, shoulders hunching as she curls in on herself on the bed.

I slide the covers out from under her and climb in, then wrap an arm around her waist and pull her ass back against my lap. So much for not tempting myself.

I keep my arm firmly around her waist, my body molded around the outside of hers. If she moves, I'll feel it. No way she's going to escape during the night. I'm not a deep sleeper.

"You so much as move a muscle without permission and there will be hell to pay. *Capiche*?"

"Yes, sir," she murmurs.

"Huh." It must be a sexplay thing, calling me *sir*. She's way too young and casual in the rest of her speech for me to believe she regularly calls men *sir*.

"Yes, Mr. Tacone," she amends, remembering my correction earlier.

I roll her nipple between my thumb and forefinger. "Good girl." It comes out as a satisfied rumble. And I genuinely feel it.

She'd make a great pet. And I'd fucking love to be her master.

CHAPTER 4

*Caitlin*

I WAKE to the smell of pancakes and my tummy rumbles. I never got to eat what I consider the dinner of champions last night—the bowl of Golden Grahams I poured myself before I found the Tacone brother in my apartment.

I squirm around, attempting to sit up. My feet and hands are numb from having the blood cut off and my whole body aches from being forced to stay in the same position for the last twelve hours. I play the game I've been playing from the start, which is pretending I'm not a prisoner, and that this is all fun and games to me.

"I smell pancakes!" I call out with exaggerated glee.

I'm satisfied when Mr. Tacone appears in the doorway, amusement playing over his face. He looks sexy as hell in crisp shirt, open at the collar, and his perfectly ironed dress slacks. "You like pancakes, little hacker?"

"I love them," I profess. "And I'm starving. And about ready to chew my own foot off to get out of these things. Please?" I hold out my hands and put my puppy dog eyes on.

Tacone's lips twitch. He pulls the nail clippers I used yesterday out of his pocket and clips off both zip ties.

I gasp at the sensation of blood returning to my hands and feet. "Ooh oh ow!" I drop my face back into the covers and roll it back and forth, squirming around and moaning.

After a few minutes, the terrible pins and needles dissipate and I sit back up to find Mr. Tacone just standing there, watching me.

"It's your fault, you know," I shoot at him, rather than feel embarrassed of my behavior.

"I'm aware," he says mildly. A true sadist.

I admit, it turns me on.

He tips his head in the direction of the door. "Come on."

I step gingerly on my feet, gasping some more, and follow him to a modern kitchen with gleaming quartz countertops and stainless steel appliances.

A plate stacked with pancakes is on the breakfast bar. I immediately plop onto a barstool, like this is the morning after a date.

Oddly, it seems to work. He offers me a mug of coffee, then arranges three pancakes on a plate and slides it in front of me.

"Oh my God," I say, digging in without even waiting for the butter and syrup he's passing over. "I'm so hungry and this smells so good." My mouth is full now, so he may not have understood a word I said.

I look up to find him watching me, same as ever. "It's an act, right?"

"What is?"

"The crazy thing. I don't mind it. Actually, I find it cute. I just don't buy it."

My fork hovers in midair and I forget to chew. Funny that I've never been called on it before and this guy sees through me right away.

I set the fork down. "I have a disorder. Does it make me this nuts? Hard to say. How do you separate it all out?" I don't know why the hell I'm philosophizing with a mafia man who kidnapped me.

He lifts his chin at my plate. "*Mangia.*" Clearly not going to partake in the philosophizing.

"Did you eat?"

He starts like he'd forgotten about serving himself. "No." He fixes a second plate but doesn't sit down. He remains standing across from me, staring me down as he butters his cakes.

I go back to eating, hoping he'll drop the previous conversation.

He does, but he shocks me even more when he says, "I like you, Caitlin. It'd be pretty impossible not to."

I make a dissenting sound in my throat. "I know at least a thousand people who'd disagree with you on that."

He frowns, then shakes his head.

"I know there's a *but* coming."

"Oh there's definitely a *but*, sweetheart."

I suck in my breath at his brusque tone. Here it comes.

"I brought your computer and all your tech equipment. You have until 5:00 p.m. tomorrow to return the money with interest. If you comply, I'll let you walk."

I go cold all over. "I can't." I shake my head. "I don't have it. I used it for tuition."

"I know you did, doll. Yours and your brother's."

He lets that drop like an anvil between us. My fork falls out of my fingers.

He knows about Trevor. Fuck. I was hoping the fact that Trev took his adopted family's last name would keep him out of it. I was careful to funnel his money through a separate fake scholarship fund, too.

Dammit.

He just shakes his head slowly. "You don't want me to spell it out, doll. Hell, I don't want to spell it out for you. But you and I both know what I'm capable of. Right?"

My heart hammers against my ribs. I can hardly breathe. Somehow, I manage to nod.

"So get on that computer of yours and get me the money. The clock is running."

I feel like puking or crying or both at once.

This isn't good. Not at all.

It's a totally different game with Trevor's life at risk. I didn't care that much about mine. This life hasn't shown me all that much worth savoring so far. But if Trevor died because of me... well, I can't even think about that. My mind whirs on the problem.

"So how much is interest?" I don't quite manage to keep the tremor out of my voice.

"Normally we charge forty-nine percent, compounded daily. But let's just call it an even 200K."

I gulp. "200K in interest or total?"

I catch that glimmer of a smile. I wonder what he'd look like with a full smile. Somehow, I can't picture it. It would probably crack his face. "Two hundred total."

I spread my hands on the table. "I need more time," I tell him firmly. "The scam I set up on the Bellissimo was a fifth of a penny on every transaction. The money accrued slowly, day by day. I didn't just siphon off two hundred grand. That would've gotten me caught six years ago."

He lifts his shoulders. "I'm sure you'll figure something out."

"*More time*," I insist. I know it's crazy that I think he'll negotiate with me, but well, we've been doing crazy things. And he did make me pancakes.

"Sorry, doll. Get me the money, dropped into your offshore account. I'll handle transferring and washing it from there." My heart sinks even further, because I'd been considering the very stupid idea of framing him for whatever money I steal.

"And don't even think about not delivering or messaging for help or anything that will piss me off, *bella*." He holds up his phone and I see a video of my brother walking out of his dorm, books tucked under his arm. "I have a guy on him now."

My stomach sinks to the floor and I suddenly wish I'd skipped the pancake I already ate. I push the plate with the other two away.

I'm not going to get away with this. You can't steal that much money in a short period of time. Not in the ways I've worked out, anyway. Even if I could infiltrate the account system of every casino in Vegas—which I would need months to do—I'm still not even sure I'd rack up the two hundred grand in thirty-one hours.

Fuck.

So basically, I'm going to go down for this.

I guess it's better than the alternative, which is Trevor getting killed for my stupidity.

I fix my hitman with a glare. "Laptop?"

He arches a brow. "Don't get bitchy, little girl. We still have to be together for two days."

I make a snorting sound, but he's right. We do. And I definitely liked the kinder, gentler side he showed me. I mean, there were moments: the jacket in the trunk of the car. The bath. Pancakes.

Oh God, am I trying to put icing on a cake made out of shit? I'm nuttier than they say.

He clears my plate and lifts his chin in the direction of the dining room. I look over and see all my tech stuff set up—everything from my apartment, including highly illegal blockers and re-routers to keep my identity and location from being discovered.

I get up and pad to the table in the dining room where I sit down and flick the switches on my equipment. I open the lid of my laptop and stare at the screen, which is as blank as my mind.

Crap! Who am I going to steal the money from? Especially if I'm sure to get caught, it seems like I ought to have an agenda for it. Like the Tacones killed my dad. I don't have any other huge personal vendettas, but maybe I could invent one.

I certainly hate Dr. Alden, my graduate advisor.

But he wouldn't have two hundred grand available to steal. Maybe I could frame him for the crime, though.

But it needs to be a large corporation. Maybe it's best to stick with Las Vegas casinos. They're raping their customers anyway, right? So which one?

I pull up a map of the strip and stare at it, but my thoughts whirl around Trevor. How to keep him safe. If there's any way out of this for me.

Not arriving at any plan that doesn't leave us dead or hunted for the rest of our lives, I swallow down the bile and choose a large casino at random. The Luxor will work. I start the tedious job of hacking in through their security walls.

Three hours later, I'm stiff and restless. I crack my knuckles and shake my hands out. I beat my fists on my deadened thighs. I need some heavy exercise to bring me back into my body. I should be on my bike right now, riding between the classes I'm missing.

I look over at my captor, who sits on the couch reading the newspaper. Babysitting me. I wonder if he'd let me out for a run? Put me on a leash like a dog—

Now I'm turned on.

I remember all the things he did to me last night. The glorious whipping. The way he stuffed his cock in my mouth. Even the anal. They all made the top of my list of sexual experiences. And my list was fairly long to begin with. Starting with the ones I never want to remember.

I want to hate my hitman. Not for the things we did but for threatening my brother. And I do.

Especially because he could be the guy who killed my dad.

*Was he a thief like you?*

Those words hit too close to home. My dad was always putting the hustle on someone. He probably did steal from the Tacones. He might have deserved what he got.

Does that make me hate them any less?

No. Not the faceless Tacone family. But the man across the room?

Sort of.

*I like you, Caitlin. It'd be pretty impossible not to.*

Well, fuck him. I wasn't looking for him to like me. I definitely don't like him.

Except that's a lie. I'm attracted to this guy like a super magnet. And even though this has been traumatic, it's also sort of addictive. I feel more alive. Awakened. Present.

I steal a glance at him. Still sexy as hell. He has this brutal ruggedness to his energy and face that doesn't match the thousand dollar suit and shiny shoes. Not that he doesn't wear them well—he does. But I could just as easily see him in the cheap suit and gold chains with a pair of brass knuckles over his fingers.

And none of that does anything to lessen my attraction to him.

Which is nuts.

I don't even know which Tacone he is. I should at least know that much.

I shake my fingers out again and pull up a new screen. It would be much more fun to hack the Chicago Police database.

*Paolo*

THE LITTLE HACKER'S been at it all morning, fingers flying over the keys, glasses pushed up on her nose.

She's damn cute. I still regret threatening her. I liked things better before she went pale and pissed. Before I brought her brother into things.

But it had to be done. I can't let her get away with stealing from us just because she makes me smile and gives good head.

Still, I find myself already wanting to make it up to her. Once she pays me back, that is.

Figuring out if there's any favor I might do for her. Because she certainly didn't have to offer up that sweet little body of hers the second she saw me sitting in her apartment.

Fuck, does she do that often?

The thought sends unease crawling over my skin. Not jealousy, although I do strangely feel that. But I'm suddenly worried for her well-being. If she just surrenders to any and every guy who shows up wanting something from her, she could get hurt—badly.

Hell, she's already been hurt badly.

That much is obvious. The girl wasn't born this twisted. Something—or more likely some*one*—made her this way. And I suddenly have the urge to beat that someone to a bloody pulp.

*Nobody* lays a hand on this girl without her wanting it.

Trouble is, she may always want it.

I sit back and drink her in. She's still in nothing but my

t-shirt, sitting right where I put her, working away. Her long, pale legs are curled under the chair, one foot twitching against the other. Her fingers have slowed down on the frantic typing. I peer to see the screen.

What the fuck?

A mug shot of me is up. My literal mugshot. I got arrested once for aggravated assault after I gave a beat-down to a drug dealer who'd moved into the neighborhood twenty-some years ago. Of course, no charges were pressed and cops had to let me go.

I stand up and walk up behind Caitlin to look closer. She's reading my rap sheet. A couple misdemeanors. Nothing that ever stuck.

I wrap my fist in her hair and tug her head back, leaning over to put my face beside hers. "What. The fuck. Are you doing, little girl?"

"Figuring out which brother you are. You wouldn't tell me." She offers it up so innocently. Like it's perfectly normal to hack into the Chicago Police files and retrieve people's records to find out their first names. I guess it would've been easier for her if I did Facebook.

I'm not a laugher. I don't even smile much. But somewhere deep inside me, far from coming out, I'm laughing.

This girl is such a nutjob.

"So it's Paolo, right?" She tries to turn her head, but my grip on her hair stops the movement. "Or do you go by Pauly?"

I can't hold back the snort. "It's still Mr. Tacone to you, doll. And right now I'd better be hearing *I'm so sorry, Mr. Tacone*, because you are not on task, little hacker. I ought to whip your ass again for this."

I didn't mean it. I don't feel one shred of anger or violence toward her. I'm the kinda guy who's used to making threats to get his point across. But she slides her gaze sideways to see my face and with the naughtiest expression possible says, "Please?"

For one moment I go still, making sure I'm interpreting that correctly.

Then I let out a puff of laughter. Just one puff, but it actually comes out of me.

I pull her to her feet and bend her over that dining room table so fast she gasps. My cock is hard when I pin her wrists behind her back and hold them with one hand. With the other, I yank my belt out of the loops.

She lets out a small warbling sound.

I'm pretty sure it's excitement.

I don't hold back. Last night I held back and she told me she could've taken more. This time I pull up the hem of her shirt to bare her ass and let my belt swing.

She squeals and lifts one foot from the floor.

I whip her again.

This time she's ready. She holds perfectly still. I let her have it, striping her ass with rapid, heavy strokes that make her dance and gasp. Welts rise across her pale cheeks. I keep going. Her whole ass turns a rosy red.

When it looks painful enough, I stop.

"More." Her voice is small, almost like she doesn't want to say it.

I hesitate. I don't really want to give her more. If I keep going, the pretty blush will turn into something purple and angry-looking and then it will stop being sexy and my conscience will have a hard time with what I've done.

I drop the belt and smack her with my palm, instead.

I swear she gives a blissful sigh and her upper body relaxes on the table. She pushes her ass out more.

Spanking her with my hand is pleasurable. I like the feel of her soft flesh under my palm, the warmth and give of it. The slight sting I receive in return. More than that, though, I enjoy the whole act. Dominating her.

It's what I do naturally—who I am. I am my father's son, no doubt about that. I'm the guy in charge. Always. With women I keep it dialed way back, but they see it anyway. It makes them run for cover. But not this one. My aggression makes her hum. Turns her on.

She widens her legs and gives me the full view of her gleaming pussy, dewy and plump.

My cock tents my trousers, hard and thick. I'm dying to pound into her, especially when she's showing me that pretty pussy and I can see her readiness.

I stop spanking and pull her up, then force her to the carpet on her knees.

She orients herself to my crotch and reaches for the button on my pants.

"Good girl," I praise. Because she really is. A very good bad girl. "But that wasn't what I had in mind." I drop to my knees, too and pull my t-shirt off her body, leaving her gloriously naked. She's so beautiful, I could stare at her body for hours. It's not perfect. One breast is larger than the other. Her belly has a little paunch to it despite how toned the rest of her is. And I love all of it. Everything that makes her unique and imperfect and real.

"Turn around, doll."

She gets it. She quickly reorients herself away from me, on her hands and knees.

I grip her waist. "Drop those tits down to the floor." I'm not usually this disrespectful with women. She brings it out in me, I guess. She showed me her freak flag and I'm showing my *stronzo*.

A match made in hell, for sure.

I free my raging erection and roll on a condom. Somehow I have control enough to take a mental picture of what's in front of me. Her submissive pose and spanked red ass do something to me. Turn me inside out. Upside down. Make me feel like a king.

This woman is… I don't know, a unicorn. Some mythical creature no one believes exists.

Except there are men who know she exists, men who came before me and I'm just fucking positive they didn't appreciate what she is. If they had, they never would've let her go.

And that pisses me off.

I give my head a shake.

*Cristo.*

When is the last time I've thought this much about any woman?

Never.

This beautiful trainwreck is wrecking me.

I slap her ass a few more times before I bring the head of my cock to her entrance and rub. She opens for me and I slide right in. The angle is perfect. I'm balls deep looking down the slope of her slender back to her face pressed into my carpet. Her eyes are closed, lips parted. She's already in ecstasy.

Unicorn.

I fuck her slowly at first, savoring every sweet stroke of my cock inside her, the way her internal muscles contract and release like she's teasing me. Like she remembered I like it.

"That's it, *bella*. You squeeze that tight pussy around my cock. Make me feel like a real man." She squeezes harder. I groan. *Loud.* "Good girl. That's so good."

I'm already losing my cool. That's how incredible her pussy feels. The aggression in me grows. I grip her hips and slide most of the way out, then slam home with a force that wrings a sound from her. I repeat. Then pick up my speed.

She starts to moan and mewl, her cries both needy and encouraging. I stay put and use my hold on her hips to move her in and out, on my dick and away. Her dark mane ripples on the carpet with the movement, she's panting, spreading her knees wider, taking me ever-so-deep. My balls draw up tight.

"That's it, doll. Take it," I growl. I don't want to come, but it's too urgent now. It feels so fucking good. I thrust in and out, pulling her body back to meet mine.

"Oh my God!" she cries.

"That's right," I taunt, like I'm the God and not just some asshole taking advantage of the sweetest offering he's ever encountered.

I come.

She doesn't.

Dammit.

I reach around and find her clit piercing and rub but

she still doesn't go off. Feeling an urgency to bring her to completion, I pull out the second I stop shooting my load and yank her ass back on my lap. I spread her legs over my knees and start spanking her pussy.

Over and over again I spank, quick stinging spanks right over her clit until she screams and arches those uneven tits in the air and yanks my hand over her mons. I sink a couple fingers into her to feel the squeezing of her channel while I grip that whole pussy tight.

Like it belongs to me.

Like I'm never gonna let it go.

Even when she's done coming, I still don't let it go.

Not until her exhaled breaths become shaky and broken. Not until I realize she's crying.

"Aw fuck, doll," I murmur, releasing her pussy and pulling her tighter into my lap. "Are you okay? Did I hurt you?"

"No." To my surprise, she doesn't pull away, but instead tucks her face into my neck, wetting my skin with her tears. I pick her up and carry her to the couch, where I sit down with her in my lap.

I stroke my palm down her leg and realize she has a killer set of rug burns on her knees. I circle each one with my index finger. "I'm sorry," I murmur.

I'm not one to apologize. Ever. I'm the dick who'd rather cut off his own finger than apologize, but I say it. And I mean it.

I don't ever want to hurt her in a way she doesn't like.

That's the sweet truth of *La Madonna*.

I grip the back of her head and pull it away from my neck to see her face.

Oh fuck.

I run my thumb over the bright patch of skin on her cheek.

"Do I have rug burn?"

"Yeah, doll."

A fresh round of tears start up.

I don't freak. She said she wasn't hurt. She isn't pulling away. She's a quirky girl. She laughs when she should run. Surrenders when she should fight. Maybe she cries when she feels good. What do I know?

I grab a blanket off the back of the couch. It's one of those soft chenille things, in red. I never use it, but the decorator bought it when she furnished the home. I wrap it around her and lean back to hold her.

"Did I break you, or is this part of the Wylde West?"

She lets out a watery laugh. "It's just the release. Maybe the start of sub drop, I don't know."

"What's that?"

"It's the endorphin crash after an adrenaline rush. It can happen after a particularly big scene."

*A scene.* That's a new way to look at sex. I trace the outline of her face, staying away from the rug burn. Burrow my fingers in her hair behind her head and pull her face up to mine.

Her eyes widen in shock. Of all the things I've done to her, a kiss is what surprises her most. I'm gentle tasting her lips, gliding mine across hers. She remains still at first, although I swear I sense her heart pounding. Like it's this act of intimacy that spikes her adrenaline most of all.

Sweet little unicorn.

I deepen the kiss.

She draws in a shuddery breath and then wraps her arms around my neck and kisses me back. Full package kiss—tongue, lips, beaded nipples turning to my chest.

I drop one hand to cup her breast, rubbing my thumb over the taut nipple. When we break the kiss, I say, "Jesus, you're sweet."

"Sweet but psycho," she says, like that's her theme song. She pushes off my lap and stands up. "But you don't seem to mind." She cups her red ass and gives her hair a toss as she sashays out of the living room, into my bedroom. I hear the bathroom door close.

I should keep closer tabs on her.

Follow her in there to make sure she doesn't arm herself.

Except I'm certain she'd never win a fight with me. *Maybe* with the help of a gun, but that's still a big maybe. I have plenty of practice disarming would-be heroes. So I leave her be.

She deserves some privacy and a break after the way I just gave it to her.

And I don't have it in me to be any more of an asshole to her than I've already been.

∽

*Caitlin*

Wow. Just wow. That's all.

I feel incredible. The sub drop lifted. Maybe it wasn't

sub drop—maybe it was just one of those orgasms that makes you cry—is that the same thing? I don't know.

All I know is that I feel great now.

Starving, but great.

Every cell in my body is alive. Tingling. My body is sated, but I still feel sexy as hell. Beautiful, even.

I blink at myself in the mirror. The rug burn on my cheek is going to turn into a bright raspberry. That's too bad. But no biggie. I don't mind wearing sex badges as proof of my accomplishments. If only they made those Girl Scout patches—I'd be all over collecting them.

I cup my breasts and gaze back at my reflection. My skin is flushed, my eyes are bright.

I look… happy.

Hell, I feel happy.

Which I know is wrong. I have problems that can't be fixed by good sex.

I'm going to go to jail.

It's either that or my brother gets hurt by the man I took as a lover.

Except I'm finding it hard to believe he would hurt me. Or my brother. Oh, I'm sure he's quite capable of it. I'm sure he does such things on a regular basis. But he just let me cry on his neck without blinking an eye. Without getting weird and pushing me away. Without judging me.

And now that I think about it, that might be the source of my current buoyancy.

It's like I've been *received*—crazy and all—for the first time in my life. I've had doms provide aftercare during sub-drop before, but they still kept a distance. Or they were overly tender.

Paolo just accepted it. Didn't make it a big deal.

And then he kissed me.

I look for a brush, but all Paolo has is a comb. I'll never get it through the tangled mess that is my hair right now.

The door opens. As if Paolo read my mind, he plops my giant satchel purse on the counter. "I grabbed your toothbrush and shit from your place," he says. "It's all in there."

I tip my head to the side. "Because this is just a big sleepover?"

His lips twitch. I seriously want to figure out how to make the guy smile. He catches my wrists and pulls me up against his hard body. My breath goes out with a whoosh. My knees go weak. "You know what you have to do, little hacker. Get me my money. Then I'll take you home. Just like that."

My heart hammers at my chest. "Just like that," I repeat at a murmur.

"I'll even let you ride in the front seat instead of the trunk. It doesn't have to be hard."

"Can I drive?"

"No chance."

"Kidding. I don't know how to drive, anyway." One of the perks of hitting driving age without a parent. I blink up at him. "I need *more time*, Paolo," I plead. "Let me pay it over time. Tack on more interest. Please?"

He shakes his head. "Sorry, doll. End of tomorrow is your deadline. You didn't come to me for a loan. You stole from me. Only reason I'm not putting the hurt on is because you're so fucking adorable."

I'm not sure why that makes me blush.

My reaction is ridiculous. Who cares if he thinks I'm adorable? My life is essentially over now.

And it's his fault.

Except I know that's not exactly true. It's my own damn fault. And it was probably my dad's damn fault for getting himself killed, too. I guess it runs in the family. Thank God Trevor seems to have missed out on the stupid gene.

My stomach grumbles.

"You hungry? What do you want for lunch?"

Well, if he's asking... "Are you too Italian for take-out pizza?"

He grins. A real, genuine grin. Short-lived, but I saw it. "I'll do pizza. What do you like on it?

"Sausage and jalapeño." I lift my chin in challenge to my strange request and the grin reappears for a flash.

"I might be too Italian for that. Nah, I can deal. Sausage and jalapeño it is. I don't need to tie you up and cover your mouth with tape when the delivery boy gets here, right?"

I shrug, affecting a sort of interested look. "Well, I've never had two doms at once, but I'm definitely interested in trying."

Of all the things I've done to shock him—and yeah, I can admit it—I do use the crazy thing for effect, this is the one that he actually responds to. His brows slam down and he wraps one meaty palm around my throat. He doesn't use it to squeeze, but he holds me in place. His forehead drops down to mine. "I don't share, doll. Remember that."

A shiver runs through me and my pussy clenches. "Noted."

He releases my throat and runs his thumb down the goosebumps on my arm. "I washed your clothes. They're on the bed."

He washed my clothes. Is it just me or does this hitman seem awfully domesticated? Pancakes? Clothes washing? I'm having a hard time assimilating it all.

And that might be the understatement of the year.

I search through my bag and find the toothbrush, my hairbrush and my cosmetic bag. Did he think I'd want to put on makeup for him while he holds me prisoner and threatens my brother's life?

Clearly.

And I think I will. I step into the shower even though I had a bath last night. I want to wash and condition my hair and rinse off the carpet dust.

Not that his carpet wasn't perfectly new, fluffy and clean. It was. Is. Whatever.

I turn on the spray of water, enjoying the renewal of pain when the warm water hits my whipped ass and the rug burns.

Ahhhh, yes. The sensations that ground me.

*Paolo*

CAITLIN STAYS in the bathroom a full forty-five minutes.

She might have stayed there all day, but I call her when the pizza arrives.

She comes out looking adorable in her workout clothes, her hair wet, her lips that bright pink candy gloss.

"How is it? Did you try it?" She scrunches her hair as she walks toward me. Her wide mouth is stretched in a smile. I'm pretty sure she does this on purpose—acts like we're the oldest friends—to manage her fears. Or to manage me. Not sure which.

Either way, I don't mind it. I enjoy it, in fact.

I think she's cute on wheels.

She comes over and scoops a piece of pizza out of the box with her hands and takes a bite. I offer her a plate but she's not stopping to rest. The girl eats that whole slice standing up in my kitchen, without coming up for air.

Well, that's what college students do.

She takes a second slice out of the box and tosses it on the plate, then walks back to her computer.

"Want me to delete your police record?" she asks with her mouth full.

I hesitate. Having a hacker at my disposal is damn appealing. What else could we hack? The FBI? I'd love to see what they've collected on the Family over the years.

But I shake my head. It's not worth the risk. That's what Nico's been trying to tell us for the last five years. We can do things legally now. We have money.

"No, little hack. Work on getting me my money."

"I am." The slightly defensive tone to her voice amuses me. It's more petulant than rude. Like she fully acknowledges I'm the boss of her. And that makes my dick hard.

She clicks on the keyboard, then adjusts her glasses on

her nose and leans forward, like there's something on her screen worth attending to.

Her fingers fly over the keys again and she's at it for several more hours. Who knew hacking took so long? Maybe she really can't get it done in two days. Or maybe she's just stalling. Hard to say. I guess I'll know soon enough.

I turn on the television and scroll through the channels, pausing on some kind of action movie with Bruce Willis.

"Oh my God, that's *R.E.D.* I love this movie!" Caitlin surges to her feet, unplugs her computer and brings it to the couch, plopping down beside me. *Right* beside me, like she's my girlfriend and we're going to snuggle. I know it's conscious, these quirks of hers. When I asked her if the crazy was an act, I saw the answer on her face. It definitely is. Some kind of defense mechanism.

So, like almost everything she's thrown my way, I run with it and loop my arm over her shoulders to draw her even closer as we both divide our attention between her computer screen and the television.

Not surprisingly, she's an excellent multi-tasker, working steadily on her computer while watching the movie.

She works all the way through the movie and halfway through the next before she gives a sigh and pushes her glasses up on her nose. "I'm in. You want the money in my account?"

"That's right," I say. Vlad, my *bratva* brother-in-law, knows how to move money around and make it untraceable. He's the one we called in to trace our losses to Caitlin's off-shore account and then finally to the payments made to Northwestern and some dummy scholarship fund.

She nods, all business now. She works for another forty-five minutes and then falls back.

"Is it done?"

"Yes. Well, no, not yet. It's set up. I diverted all their transactions for the next day and a half to my account." She lifts those cornflower blue eyes to my face. "Hopefully it will be enough."

My heart starts beating faster, almost like it's in tune with hers. She's breathless, afraid.

I can't tell her I'll take anything less than what she owes me, but it's getting harder and harder to keep the pressure on.

After the way she keeps offering that hot little body up to me, I almost feel like I'm in the deficit to her. I find myself wanting to figure out how I can give something back. Something besides pizza and an orgasm.

But I'm not going to let a woman turn me soft. She stole from my family, she'll have to pay the price.

She looks away when I don't answer, then stands up. "I need exercise," she declares, like she's on some kind of holiday and gets to follow her own itinerary.

I don't know why I find it so damn appealing.

"You can work out in my gym," I tell her. "Want to lift some weights?"

She gives me a wary look. "Um, okay. Sure."

I stand and lead her to my home gym in the back of the house. The winter sun streams in through the windows. I go to shut the shades, but she exclaims, "Oh leave them open. I love the sun."

"Of course you do," I mutter. Because she's as bright as that ball of fire. The kind of sun that is way too much to look at, the kind that scorches.

I'm already certain she's burning her imprint into me.

Not sure I want to let her go.

∽

*Caitlin*

LIFTING weights is not my idea of a workout. I need cardio—I like to move to rhythm, get my heart rate up to music.

But beggars can't be choosers.

The trouble is, I don't really know what to do with any of this equipment. I bend over and try to pick up a dumbbell.

"Hang on, doll—"

I nearly break my back lifting it. It comes off the floor a half inch and crashes back down.

"Right. Too heavy." I swivel to eye Paolo's broad shoulders with new appreciation. No wonder he's so strong. He's in here lifting weights as heavy as a Mack truck.

His lips curl. It's not quite a smile, but close. He saunters over and takes the weights off the ends of the bar, leaving only the two end pieces on. "Try it this way," he says.

"That's just a bar." Oh. And it's still plenty heavy. I change my grip and do ten two-handed curls with it, then groan as I drop it back down. "I don't think this is going to work, Paolo."

His lips twitch again. "Mr. Tacone to you."

I lean into one hip and curl my hair around my finger. "I know."

The element of danger is always there with this guy, which is perhaps why I enjoy ribbing him—flirting for me —so much. I get a thrill straight to the soles of my feet every time I dare. And of course I dare every time.

His gaze on me is anything but dangerous now, though. Sure, there are traces of hunger in it, but there's actually warmth in his eyes. Indulgence.

He likes me.

For the first time in years, maybe ever, I'm starting to feel less broken. More special. It's a strange experience for someone who's been considered cray-cray for so long. All this time I sort of thought I was trying to hide my crazy from the world.

He made me realize it might be the other way around. I've been trying to hide my sanity. Because being sane in this world is too perfectly painful.

I would have to own up to all the shit that happened to me after my dad's death, and I don't want to do that.

He lifts his chin toward the treadmill. "You could run on that."

"Oh," I say brightly. "Right." I've actually never used a treadmill, but it must be easy enough. I step on and flip switches.

Paolo comes up and stands on it behind me. "Hang on, speedy." His warmth is at my back, arms reach around me to adjust settings. I push my ass back into him, and with nothing but yoga pants on, his heat bleeds right through. I like the way it feels to have him near me.

Safe.

Of course, the opposite is true.

Which makes it all the more exciting.

And now I'm back to believing I'm genuinely nutso.

Paolo steps off the treadmill and starts it. "How's that speed?"

I start walking briskly. "Perfect." I'm already smiling.

He crosses his arms over his chest.

"Are you just going to stand there and watch me?"

"Yeah. I think I am."

My smile grows bigger. "Because you think I'm cute?"

Ha—I did it! A genuine smile splits his face. "Yeah, doll. Exactly."

I keep smiling.

"So, how did you become a hacker? I'm guessing they don't exactly teach that in school?"

"No, I'm self-taught. My dad picked the occupation for me, actually. He decided it would benefit him greatly if he had a kid who could get through alarm systems or rob online banks. He stole a laptop for me when I was eleven and brought me to this guy's sketchy apartment to learn how to access the dark web."

Paolo's body goes taut and I have to rewind what I said that made him tense up.

*Oh*. The guy's sketchy apartment.

"Nothing bad happened there," I reassure him, although I don't know why I should. The bad shit happened to me *after* my dad died. After he was *murdered* by the Tacones.

So I tell it to him straight. "After my dad was murdered, life sucked. I needed a super power and hacking seemed like the answer. Foster parents can't take away your personal belongings and that laptop was mine. I used the hell out of it. I devoted every free minute I had to learning how to get past firewalls and hacking passwords. I started taking money for small hack jobs by the time I was sixteen. It helped me feel like I was capable of filing for emancipation and living on my own."

"It *is* a super power, doll. Believe me, I'm tempted to exploit the hell out of it, but I'm trying to stay clean. *Ish*. The Family's gone legit."

The Family's gone legit. That comes as news to me, but considering the money I've seen pumping through those Bellissimo accounts, I guess they don't need to resort to extortion and loan-sharking anymore. They have more money than they can spend.

"So why even study computer science? Don't you already know everything you need to know?"

I give him a wry grin. "I was trying to go legit, too. *Ish*. Too bad you're screwing that up."

He folds his arms over his burly bear chest and shakes his head. "Don't blame me for applying consequences to your misdeeds."

It's unfortunate that my kinky side finds his enforcement so panty-melting.

I stay on that treadmill, images of all the dommy things he did to me flooding my brain as I heat under his watchful stare. When I'm done, I hop off and trip over to him, giving him a peck on the cheek before he knows what I'm doing.

"When this is all over, do you think we'll be friends? Lovers? Go out on a date?" I'm play-acting. Doing the overly-familiar crazy girl thing.

But I suddenly wish I hadn't asked the questions because I realize the answer might hurt me.

Genuinely hurt me.

I'm used to losing guys after a couple dates. I'm used to driving them away with my quirks and kinks and crazy.

And this isn't a guy I'm dating or even want to date in the future.

He's a Tacone, for Christ's sake. His family killed my father. He's a hitman who's threatening my life and the life of my brother.

But I find I do care about his answer. I care very much.

Especially when a strange look comes over his face. It's the first time I've shocked him, and I've tried at least a dozen times before.

"Of course we won't," I answer for him. "Nevermind." I speed away, out of the room and when he lets me go, I know that I correctly guessed the answer.

And I hate what that knowledge does to my chest. The uneasy nervous edge that pushes into where warmth had been before.

I go back to his living room and turn on the television like it's my home, opening Netflix and putting on my new binge watch series, *Jane the Virgin.* I'm in season four.

I don't move from the couch for the rest of the afternoon into the evening. Not even when he orders in a nice dinner from a steakhouse and opens a bottle of wine.

He doesn't make me—he just brings the food to the couch and hands it to me.

I think I half want him to. To take the remote, turn the TV off and take charge of me. Make me sit across from him at the table and pretend this is a date.

But I guess he's not interested in that.

In me.

Of course he's not. He was just happy to get his dick wet while he makes sure I return the money I stole.

For me to read anything else into this is insane.

Which of course, I am.

## CHAPTER 5

*P*aolo

"THE MONEY'S THERE? And you're diverting it?" I'm on the phone with my brother-in-law Vlad to verify Caitlin's report that the money transfer has begun. Vlad is the *bratva* asshole who kidnapped my sister last year in his own revenge-slash-extortion attempt against the Tacones.

Lucky for him, or for her, or maybe for all of us, our baby sister is a unicorn in her own right. Vlad fell in love and ended up donating a kidney to save her life and calling us to bring her home. And that's the only reason he's not a dead man.

"Yes. Our side should be masked, but hers will not be. The feds will eventually trace the loss to her, same as I did when she stole from the Bellissimo."

I try to ignore the pang that gives my conscience. She made her own bed. This isn't my problem.

I rub my face. "Is there anything you can do... to, ah, slow that process down?"

"Why?" Vlad asks.

I don't answer.

"You like this girl? I saw the picture. She's pretty, no?"

Not pretty. Off-the-charts hot. "Answer the fucking question, Vlad," I snarl.

"*Nyet.* There is nothing. It's too late."

Fuck. "All right, thanks. Track the income for me and let me know when it reaches two hundred grand."

"*Da.*"

"*Grazie,*" I say back. If he's going to speak Russian, I'll speak Italian.

I get off the phone and bump into my little hacker, brushing her teeth in the hallway, listening in.

"Finish up and get in bed," I command, lifting my chin in the direction of my bedroom. As always, she's docile and obedient. It doesn't mean I let my guard down. I zip tie her hands and feet again at night.

She's been quiet ever since she asked if we'd be friends, which is doing all kinds of crazy things to my chest.

Is she actually... hurt? Insecure?

Or was she just censoring herself—kicking herself for asking when she knows I'm trouble? That she should never even speak my name again after these forty-eight hours are up.

What disturbs me is my reaction to her unease. I'm itchy, like something's wrong and I need to fix it.

Like I need to say something to soothe her hurt feelings, or ease her mind.

Except I don't know what the fuck is going on in that brilliant, beautiful head of hers.

I secure her wrists to the headboard of the bed and slide her glasses off her face to set them on the bedside table.

"Most times I'm in this position my clothes are off," she tells me.

I know it's a dare.

I know I should resist.

She's already under my skin. I fear I'm under hers.

But my dick thickens as my mind automatically strips her of her clothing. I stare down at her for a moment, considering.

We lock gazes. Hers is open. Not trusting but certainly willing to receive whatever I want to give. The position probably evoked her surrender, something she's practiced in those "scenes" she mentioned. It put her in the mood.

Even as I tell myself to walk away, I reach out and tweak one of her nipples through her sports bra.

She arches, asking for more.

"If I take off those clothes, little girl, you'll be subject to my will all night long. I'm gonna wear you out before I sleep. Wake you in the middle of the night. Fuck you hard in the morning."

Her pupils dilate. The nipple I didn't tweak beads up to match the first. She says nothing. Not a word to dissuade me.

*Cazzo*.

"You got three seconds to tell me no, little hacker. Otherwise I'll strip you naked and take you as long and hard as I please."

She sucks her lower lip into her mouth, drags her teeth across it.

Still not a sound.

"One... two... three." I unclip the zip ties and the padding beneath them and undress her. "Beautiful girl," I murmur, reattaching the underwraps and zip ties. I lower my mouth to one of her nipples and flick my tongue over it. Graze it with my teeth. Suck hard until she cries out and arches. All the while, I roll and pinch the other nipple between my fingers.

I switch sides.

Her legs grow restless, sliding up and down over the bedsheets, kicking the covers I pulled down before I strung her up.

"Fuck me, Paolo. Put that big Italian cock in me."

I slap her breast. She pants, excitement flaring in her eyes. I slap it again. "What did I tell you to call me?"

"Mr. Tacone," she purrs it, like she's thrilled I'm asking. Maybe she's hoping I'll punish her.

That thought gets my dick even harder.

*Fanculo.*

I climb off her and strip out of my clothes. She watches with avid interest, pulling that lower lip into her mouth again.

"Do I take orders from you, doll?" I ask when I straddle her, walking on my knees toward her head.

Her eyes widen. "No, sir."

"Are you the one who tells me where to put my cock?"

"No, Mr. Tacone," she says immediately. Not like she's scared. Like she can't wait to see what happens next.

I feed my cock into her mouth, letting it bump the back of her throat.

When she gags, I pull back a little, then go in again before she's ready.

"No, little hacker. I put my cock wherever the fuck I want to put it, don't I?"

She makes a muffled sound of agreement. I love the vibration around my cock. I love the way she sucks like a good girl. Swirls her tongue around. Tries to please me even though I'm the one driving. I'm the one pushing in too far and making her eyes water.

"If I want to fuck your mouth with it, I fuck it. If I want to fuck your ass, I'm gonna fuck your ass. Right, doll?"

Another sound of agreement.

I keep at it, and while I enjoy the hell out of it, it's less about my pleasure than it is to torture her a bit, because I'm fairly certain that's what she wanted. To be abused. To have control taken from her.

And I'm gonna make sure she enjoys every second of it.

I pull out of her mouth and scoot back to grip her jaw and claim her mouth. She kisses me back with fervor, her tongue sliding over my lips, her mouth slanting over mine, lips sipping.

When she bites my lower lip, I grip her throat.

"Don't," I say when she releases it.

I mean it. I don't like to be pushed, not even by her. I don't punish her or strong-talk because she likes that. I don't want to reward. I just let her see my frown. Don't move until I'm sure it's been registered.

"I'm sorry."

I trace my thumb down between her breasts. "That's a pretty apology, little girl. I like it when you surrender."

I stop at her belly button and circle it.

She lifts her hips, urging me lower.

I scoot lower and drag my thumbs up the insides of her legs. She shivers beneath my touch, her pussy glistening in anticipation of my fingers arriving there.

I tease her, rubbing circles at the apex of her inner thighs, but not touching her pussy.

"I'll be good," she whisper-promises. Like there's anything she could say that would keep me from doing whatever the fuck I want anyway.

I nip her inner thigh, flick my tongue on a path toward her pussy, but stop before I reach it.

"Mr. Tacone. Mr. Paolo. Sir. Big guy. *Please.*"

"I like the begging." I reward her with a single flick of my tongue over her core.

She sucks in her breath. "Oh please. Oh please, oh please, oh please oh please. I'll be good. I'll be such a good girl."

I meant it when I said I liked the begging. I'm harder than marble.

Maybe I've always been on a power trip.

Maybe it's always been wrong—

Until I met this girl.

I flatten my tongue and lick a long line right up the middle of her slit.

She shivers, legs scissoring to wrap around my back. I push them back off, hold them apart as I lower my head again. Then I get to work. I use my tongue in every way possible to tease her into a frenzy, keep her on the edge of an orgasm.

When she's a babbling, writhing mess, I rise up on my knees and roll her hips so she's on her belly.

Well, she doesn't quite make it to her belly because her wrists are fastened to the headboard, so she's in a contorted, twisted position that I'm a sick fuck for loving. I slap her ass, which is still red from her whipping earlier, then burrow my thumb between her ass cheeks. "Think I should fuck your ass again tonight? Hmm?"

She's wide-eyed, alert, her gaze trained on my face, but she doesn't protest. She doesn't want it, though, I can tell.

I massage her anus as I rise up behind her and grip my cock, but after I sheath it, I plunge into her pussy, not her ass.

She moans with pleasure.

I reach up and brace my palm against the headboard and start banging her with punctuated thrusts. She makes these cute little *ung* sounds every time, bracing her own hands to keep from hitting her head each time I drive her up on the bed.

"You made a big mistake showing me this side of you, Wylde West," I growl, watching her breasts bob every time I slam in.

"Why?"

I don't pause in my rhythm, each thrust so satisfying I want to bellow my success. "When your debt is paid, I might not let you go."

She twists to look at me over her shoulder and I catch a question in her gaze. A flash of something I can't read. Vulnerability? First time she's shown me any weakness.

Because I'm not dumb enough to believe the crazy act for a minute. That's a card she plays for effect, I know that. Something to push people away or make them underestimate her.

I need to stay on my toes with this one, because there's an excellent chance that despite her sexual surrender, she's preparing a countermove that will bury me.

She comes.

When her muscles tighten and squeeze my cock, I shorten my strokes, pumping hard and fast until I come, too.

As I slow my pumping, I nestle up behind her, kiss her pale shoulder. I reach around and rub the barbell of her piercing down on her clit and she comes again, with another delicious round of dick-squeezing with her inner walls.

I kiss her neck, nip the shell of her ear.

"I like fucking you, Caitlin." Stating the obvious. But it feels like a huge admission. I'm not one to talk about feelings.

Ever.

I don't even do feelings.

But there's no denying how satisfying I find it to screw the brains out of my prisoner. And that's all about how much she enjoys it, too.

∽

*Caitlin*

. . .

Paolo pulls out and cleans up. He cuts the zip tie that fastened my wrists to the headboard, but leaves the one holding my wrists together intact, as well as the one on my ankles. And like last night, he's careful not to let me see where he puts the scissors.

We settle into the same position as last night, with his arm firmly around my waist—another form of bondage. A very pleasurable form.

"What if I wanted to face you while I sleep?" I ask with mock innocence.

He doesn't take the bait. No answer.

I listen to the sound of his breath in the darkness. "Do you have a girlfriend?"

He gives a light scoff. "No."

"Wife?"

*"No."* Now he sounds annoyed.

I already noticed he doesn't wear a ring and there's no signs of a female presence in his house, but you never know. I didn't find out enough stalking him today on the internet.

"Were you ever married?" I keep pressing. I want to know more about this man. He doesn't talk enough and even though I think I have him nailed during our sexual interactions, I'm still missing so much information about him.

"No."

"Why not?"

"Not my thing. Family. Kids. I never wanted that shit. Never been a woman I could stand long-term, either."

"What's your longest?"

"There's no longest. I don't do girlfriends."

That seems strange to me, considering how considerate he can actually be. In bed and out. I don't get it.

Some silly-girl part of me wants to believe the consideration is all for me. Like I'm something new for him.

The silly-girl has to ask, "Have you whipped a woman before?"

"You're my first."

Do I detect amusement in his tone?

He's answering my questions, that alone tells me he's receptive to me, even if I'm playing the crazy card.

"Really? Because you're, um, pretty good at it."

"Pretty good?"

"Very good. I liked it—the way you whipped me. Both times."

Damn. I sound... breathless. And eager. Why do I sound so eager? I don't care what he thinks about me. I'm not cultivating a real relationship here. I'm just digging for information on my captor.

Yeah.

I'll keep telling myself that.

His cock twitches at my ass. He shifts to cup my breast. "You'd better stop running that pretty mouth or that middle of the night fucking is going to happen sooner rather than later."

My pussy clenches on air. I wouldn't mind. This man seems to *own* my body. He just looks at it and I'm wet.

"Do you like it?"

"What?"

"Hurting me." I shouldn't put it that way. He might take it wrong. Like I'm accusing him.

He bites my shoulder. "Yeah, I like it." He's quiet for a moment. "Makes me wonder if…"

"If what?"

He strums my nipple with his thumb. "I don't know. Maybe that's why I haven't done relationships. I had to keep myself on a leash."

I close my lips around a little gasp. I *am* something new for him. My heart picks up speed.

*Don't get excited about this*, I warn myself severely. He's the enemy.

And then I have to know.

Even a crazy girl has to get real at some point.

I draw a deep breath. "Did you kill my father?" If I'm honest, this is what I was trying to figure out when I hacked into his police records.

"Definitely not," he says. The reply is so immediate that I believe him.

"Do you know who did?"

He's quiet a moment. "Even if I did, I wouldn't tell you, West. Go to sleep."

Now he's calling me *West*. Is that because he's thinking about my father?

"But you knew him? You did business with him?"

"I remember him, that's all. Stop talking."

I try to turn to face him but he tightens his hold so I can't move. "You know, don't you?"

"I don't know. I could probably find out. But that doesn't mean I'd tell you the answer."

"Because it was someone in your family who did it."

"I don't think so, Caitlin—I probably woulda known. But it's possible. I can't rule it out."

The answer both disturbs and relieves me at once. It definitely wasn't Paolo. I'm not having sex with the man who pulled the trigger. And he's been thinking about it. Which doesn't make it all better, especially if it were someone in his family who did it, but he's not as dismissive about it as he was when I first accused him.

But the swirl of unease he first stirred when he asked if my dad had stolen from them returns. The more I stew on that, the more it rings true. I remember fragments of phone conversations he had around that time. Conversations that had made me certain he was killed by the mafia when I reviewed them later. When I saw myself as the victim and my dad as the hero wrested from our family. But now I'm not so sure. Now I suddenly see everything through a different lens. My dad was a shyster. He was always trying to swindle people out of their money, looking for where he could benefit. Maybe he did bring his death on himself.

"I can't help you with your father's death," Paolo says behind me, like he's been thinking about it for a while and has finally come to a decision.

For a moment, I feel nothing. Like time stands still. And then a giant ball of emotion surges up from my chest. Grief, I guess. Not for my father's death, but for what I'd made him out to be after—some kind of good guy, not the selfish, absentee, bad example of a dad he really was. Or maybe just something that belonged to me, when I had nothing.

I try to hold it in. I close my throat and choke a little, but then it erupts. My back shakes with one sob. I hold my breath, squeeze my face up to keep the rest from escaping.

It's impossible. It bursts out of me. Tears stream down my cheeks.

Paolo turns me around and rolls me up against his chest. Holds me close and rubs my back.

I'm embarrassed and mad at myself for losing control like this, but he doesn't comment. He doesn't tell me it's okay or it's not okay. He just holds me. He massages the back of my head.

And when I realize he's not going to say anything, I let go completely. I wet his skin with my tears, I let them run and run until they run out.

And afterward, when I'm completely drained, I fall into the deepest sleep of my life.

## CHAPTER 6

*Paolo*

I LET CAITLIN SLEEP IN—BREAKING my promise to use and abuse her during the night and in the morning. Not that I didn't wake up with the most painful wood ever. Not that it didn't kill me to untangle and pull away from her lithe naked body.

My heart breaks for her.

And I didn't even believe I had a heart.

But those tears she cried last night made me want to kill every motherfucker who's ever hurt her. Only I can't. I already decided I can't avenge her father's death, even though I'm willing to kill for her. But knowing the kind of guy her dad was, knowing the circles he ran in… well, I gotta assume he had it coming.

And I might be on the same side as whoever did it. I don't think it was the Tacones. But it could've been. Or one of our allies. I would call my brothers to ask what they know, but you don't talk about shit like that on the phone. It will have to wait until I can get Junior or Gio in person.

I shower and dress, then call Vlad to have him check on the account where she's siphoning the money for us. It's up to $114K.

Good. I'm still watching for her to screw me, but so far it looks like she'll be going home relatively unscathed tonight.

I start the coffee maker and fry up a package of bacon and pull out some eggs.

I wait around for a while, but when she keeps on sleeping, I fry a couple eggs for myself and eat breakfast.

Good thing I did, because she's still sleeping at lunch time. I go in and wake her up by snipping her zip ties.

I still want to promise to fix things. I am a fixer for the family. The guy they send in to be the heavy. To use threats, or my fists, or sometimes more permanent solutions to take care of problems. It's why I'm the guy they sent to straighten out this situation with Caitlin.

But fixing things for women isn't usually my gig. I mean, I'd do it. If some guy was beating on a girl, I'd step in in a heartbeat. I live and breathe violence and I would definitely use it to keep a girl safe. But I'm sure as hell not the knight in shining armor.

But this shit with Caitlin doesn't sit right. I don't mean my retribution. I haven't hurt her in any way she didn't want to be hurt. And I won't. But she's wounded. Bent in ways I don't know can be straightened out. And that makes me want to pick through her past and punish every last fucker who hurt her.

She bounces out of bed like nothing happened, though. "Good morning, *Mr. Tacone.*" She emphasizes the Mr. Tacone part like she's making fun of me.

I slap her ass as she limps past me on her way to the bathroom. "You can call me Paolo," I concede.

She looks back, her eyes widening with exaggerated surprise. "Ooh, I graduated. How did I pass to the next level? Was it the bawling all over your chest?" She beams like bawling is something adorable.

And in her case, it suddenly is. Or rather, talking about it like it's cute makes it so.

"Something like that," I tell her.

She stops and curls her fingers between her legs, making my eyes and my dick pop. "Why am I not swollen and tender from all that pounding you promised?"

And like every time, I respond.

I'm on her in a flash, walking her backward until her ass hits the wall. "Now you're in trouble."

"Yeah, I should've waited until I peed."

"You should've," I say, but don't let go. I'm rubbing between her legs and she gets wet by the second swipe. I thrust a couple fingers inside her and she rises up on her tiptoes, her back sliding up the wall.

I'll make it fast, since she does have to pee. I have a constant boner for her, so I don't need any foreplay. Just a quick application of a condom and I'm buried deep inside her, shoving her ass up that wall with each pounding thrust.

She wraps her legs around my waist, arms around my shoulders. I fuck her until she's babbling my name, begging for release.

"Can you come on command?" I ask.

"You already know I can," she says, which is true. I found that out at her place, which seems like a million years ago.

"Then when I say come, you're gonna come, and you're gonna squeeze my cock so good I'll forget all about fucking that ass today."

"I'm ready *now.* Please now."

I watch her face as I slam in, jackhammering her into the wall, watching her need grow more and more desperate until I can't take it anymore.

"Come, Caitlin." I shove in deep and shoot my load and squeeze one of her nipples hard.

She screams and comes, her juicy pussy milking the cum from my cock until I get lightheaded from the release.

"Paolo," she murmurs as I coast in and out, stroking her through the aftermath.

Turns out I fucking love hearing my name on her lips, especially in that breathy, sexy way.

I slide out and slam in. "Say it again."

"Paolo."

I meet her eyes and see a streak of vulnerability. Right before she covers it with sass. "Now you want me to say it."

"You'll say whatever the fuck I ask you to say, right, little girl?" I bump my loins against her again.

"Do you tell all your shakedowns that?" Again, the vulnerability. She's been asking this shit a lot. She wants to know where she stands with me.

My mouth twists into a smirk. "Not from this position."

She laughs. Not a crazy laugh, but a genuine, beautiful, musical laugh.

I find myself grinning back at her—which feels fucking good, because I never grin.

I pull out and set her down. "Go pee."

"Yes, Mr. Tacone." She tosses her hair over her shoulder and blinks rapidly at me.

I smack her ass.

Cute as fuck.

I really don't want to let her go.

*~*

*Caitlin*

I DIDN'T KNOW how late I slept until I come out of the shower and find out it's already 1:40 p.m.

I sort of dash for the computer to check on the money balance. Am I even close to making the amount required by the deadline? What happens if I don't make it? Surely he'll cut me a break? He was just balls deep between my legs.

But I really don't know this guy. He's dangerous, for sure.

"Where are we?" He stands over me.

"One hundred thirty-eight."

"Getting there."

I look up at him. "Do I get a few hours leeway? You know, if it's all not there by the deadline?"

"Yeah, doll. We're good. I can see you're putting in a good faith effort here."

Good faith effort. The effort that's going to get me sent to prison for ten to twenty years.

Damn.

I go into his workout gym and get on the treadmill. I stay on it until he drags me off two hours later and I can barely stand on the stable ground.

He grips my elbows to hold me up. "We're good. Money's close enough. You can shut it off and I'll take you home."

I know my crazy is in full force when my first emotion is disappointment. Like I don't want to leave.

And that's as cray-cray as it gets.

"And my brother? He's off the hook now, too? You'll pull your guys off him?"

"No one's touched him, Caitlin. He doesn't know any of this happened." He brings his face up to mine. "No one will, right?"

"I won't talk."

"You won't do anything that will make me come look for you again. *Capiche*?"

"Yeah, I *capiche*."

"Get your shit together. I'll take you home."

I'm slightly bewildered about the sudden dismissal. I doubt we reached two hundred thousand yet, but I'm not going to complain.

Because that would be nuts.

I'm going home.

I shouldn't feel so damn disappointed.

Abandoned, even.

Man, I really am a nut-job.

Maybe it's just because I know that after this I'll be going to jail. I don't know if it will take them a week or a month or a year to trace me, but I imagine they will. Even if I spend the rest of the night trying to wipe out that bank account's existence from all records.

I pack up my stuff and Paolo takes me to the Porsche. True to his word, he lets me ride in front this time.

"So, I told you I won't help with your dad's death. But is there anything else I can do for you? Anyone whose kneecaps you want broken?"

I shoot him a sidelong glance. "What?"

He shrugs. "You heard me."

"You're serious? Why are you offering?"

"We're square now, with the money. But you took care of me quite a few times these last two days and I, uh, want to return the favor."

I blink at him. Am I actually hearing this right?

"So this is like a transaction? I sucked your cock and now you'll break someone's kneecaps for me?"

I see that twitch of his lips. "Yeah. Something like that. Does that offend you?"

"Well, I do give good head." I fall back on crazy-Caitlin because while I am slightly offended, I'm also way turned on.

"You do."

I laugh. "I can think of quite a few people I'd love to sic you on. My graduate advisor for one. But no, thank you. I'm good."

Paolo's hands tighten on the wheel. "What'd he do?"

"Oh he's just an ass. Let's just say he didn't follow through on our blowjob transaction deal."

Paolo's brows slam down. "You blew him? And what was he supposed to do for you?"

"He promised me the TA position and then gave it to someone else. But I mean it—I don't need you to hurt him. I can take care of myself. Can I get a credit for one future ass-beating when needed? Or better yet—" *Don't say it. Don't sound needy.* "Use it on myself?"

He takes his eyes off the road to look at me. He's hard to read, but I think I catch the traces of amusement in his expression. "Yeah, doll. Sure."

I'm not certain which thing he's saying yes to and I won't let myself ask. He's circling the graduate housing block where my low-rent graduate student apartment is.

"You can let me out here," I say, throwing open the door when he stops at a stop sign.

"Nah, I can— "

I'm already out the door. "Thanks for the fun times, Paolo. Catch you on the flip side." I heave my satchel over my shoulder and wave after I shut the door.

He looks at me through the glass for a beat, then lifts his chin and drives away.

I try to fight the panic chewing through my gut.

It's not because he's leaving.

It's because I'm going to jail very soon.

And that's all.

I have absolutely no feelings for Paolo Tacone at all.

That would be crazy.

## CHAPTER 7

*Paolo*

FOR THE FIRST time in my life I'm off-kilter. I don't consider myself a real emotional guy. If shit upsets me, I bang some heads and I feel better. End of story.

But this is different. It's a low-level unease. Not anger. Maybe it's my non-existent fucking conscience waking up. I didn't like letting Caitlin go, and as the days wear on, that sensation only increases.

I pay a visit to Junior and Gio, my brothers who live locally to find out if they remember anything about Lake West. Neither remembers any more than I do. The guy was shady—possibly a middle man for stolen goods—but not much else. Gio thinks he might have worked for the Russian *bratva*. Not Vlad's cell, but an older organization. One we had some uneasy ties with at one point. If that's true, it could've been one of theirs who killed him.

I keep my soldier's eyes on Trevor West for a few weeks after I let Caitlin go. And I take the job of watching Caitlin myself.

Vlad had no problem transferring and laundering the money from her account and he reported that she deleted its existence completely, which bodes well for her not getting herself caught for the crime she committed.

Still, I keep tabs on her. I like knowing she's safe. Back at school and teaching her cardio classes. Wearing the hell out of her yoga pants and t-shirts under her red puffy jacket.

I don't like the deadened expression in her eyes. What bothers me most is thinking I'm the one who put it there.

Except I can't quite make myself believe that. She found pleasure with me, I'm sure of it. She may have used sex to inure me to her, but those orgasms weren't faked.

God knows I found pleasure with her. She's an addiction. Now that she's gone, now that she's taken that aura of chaos she carries with her away, my house feels empty.

I find out her graduate advisor is a guy named Noah Alden and I pay him a visit in his office. The guy screams pompous ass from ten miles away. He's short and slovenly dressed with a paunchy belly. I'm pissed that Caitlin's lips were anywhere near this guy's junk. In fact, I want to kill him just for that. But that's not why I'm here.

I break into the guy's office and sit down in his chair to wait for him. He nearly pisses himself when he finds me there.

"Wh-what's going on here? Who are you?"

I take my time and stand from the chair, giving him a

moment to register my full size. The flash of the gun I carry in the holster under my arm. The size of my fists.

I saunter around the desk. "I'm here to discuss one of your graduate students with you."

"Wh-who is it? What is this about?"

"Why did you pass Caitlin West over for the TA position you promised her?"

His face crinkles into scorn. "Caitlin? She's crazy."

And that's all it takes. My fist slams into his nose and he slams into the wall. "Say it again," I challenge, fisting his shirt to pick him up from where he slumped down to the floor. "Go on. Call her crazy to my face. I'll fucking show you crazy."

Blood gushes down his face, spills over my hands. "I-I-I'm sorry. I didn't mean it, I swear! She's a nice girl. Real sweet. Just a little… unique, is all. Is she your girlfriend or something?"

"Something," I say, slamming him back against the wall. "Now you listen to me. You're gonna give Caitlin that TA job she deserves, or I'm gonna break every bone in both your hands. *Capiche*?"

"I-I-I can't give her the job, I already gave it to someone else."

"Yeah, I heard that. You're gonna take it back. Or I'll get rid of him and it'll be on your head. Got it?"

"Yeah, yeah, I got it."

"By tomorrow, and don't tell anyone—including Caitlin—about this conversation we're having."

"I won't. Okay, I got it."

"And if you ever disrespect that girl again, I will fucking kill you. Understand?"

"I understand. I won't disrespect her. Please."

I punch him once more in the gut to make sure he gets the message before I release him.

I stalk out, still pissed as hell.

Fucking *stronzo*—calling Caitlin crazy. People are so fucking stupid if they can't see that's all a big act to make sure people underestimate her. It's her way of controlling her surroundings from a position of weakness. Some survival skill she probably had to learn after her dad died, if not before.

∽

*Caitlin*

THE FIRST THING I did when Paolo dropped me home was go over and see Trevor. Paolo was right. He hadn't noticed anyone watching him. Didn't even register that I hadn't checked in.

I debated telling him what happened, but I decided not to worry him. He's happy. He's almost like a normal college student, partying and hooking up with girls and having fun. His existence has been different from mine. We got separated into different foster families. His adopted him. They were decent. He's turned out normal.

I don't want to disturb that.

So I go on.

Only everything's different now.

I'm different.

I keep thinking about Paolo. Wondering if I should've

played anything differently. If I made a mistake having sex with him. The old me would've beat myself up for my crazy. Wondered when I'm ever going to be normal. Not turn to sex and pain to get through stressful situations.

New me can't find it in me to condemn myself. I don't feel dirty or cheap or used.

I feel satisfied. Satisfied enough to wonder at least ten times a day if I'll ever see Paolo again. If he's into having sex or scening with me again. Maybe meeting up at the BDSM dungeon. Or at his place.

And I keep replaying his offer. The way we left things. That I could call in a favor if I needed one. And he didn't give me his phone number or anything, but I'm a hacker. I could find it easily enough.

But all those thoughts are pretty pointless when I remember that any day now the FBI could show up at my door to arrest me.

I go into my graduate advisor, Dr. Alden's office after he left me a message saying he needed to meet with me.

The minute I see him a flood of hot and cold rush through me. Both his eyes are black and there's tape across his nose.

Paolo's been here.

Oh my God.

I should feel guilty, but I guess I'm immoral enough that I don't. All I feel is vindicated.

And something else—some part of me is celebrating.
*Paolo does care.*

"What happened?" I try to make my voice sound normal.

"I ran into the door," he says in the strained voice that confirms everything.

I pull out a chair and sit down, my heart thudding. "You wanted to see me?"

"Yeah, uh, listen. We had a situation come up. Todd can't do the TA job anymore and I wanted to see if you could step in. This semester—right away."

"Oh, uh... yeah. I could do that." I try to sound surprised, natural. But who am I kidding? We both know what happened here.

"Great. Here's everything you need." He pushes a stack of papers across the desk at me. "Be ready to teach tomorrow."

"All right. I will. Thanks." I stand.

Well, hot damn. That's $15,000 a year, which I will definitely need since I don't have the Tacone money coming in any more.

I leave the office, debating whether I should try to contact Paolo to thank him.

No, I should leave it alone. We had sex while he held me prisoner. This isn't some romantic gesture. It's probably considered sociopathic.

I'm getting on my bike when I get that feeling I've had lately that I'm being watched.

I thought it was me being paranoid about the FBI showing up to arrest me, but I suddenly realize it might be Paolo. I scan the streets. No sign of the Porsche.

But there. I see a dark blue Range Rover parked on the street across the way with a large figure behind the wheel.

I can't stop the smile spreading across my face.

And suddenly I'm lighter than a helium balloon. I sail

across the street, open the passenger door and scoot into the seat, uninvited. "You missed me!" I sing out. "So, *are* we dating now?"

His face is inscrutable, as usual, except I catch the twitch of his lips that tells me he doesn't mind my crazy.

I lean across the console to peck him on the cheek, but he turns and catches my jaw in his large hand and stays my approach.

My pussy squeezes at the dominant hold. His grip isn't painful, just controlling. He holds my face immobile and studies it. "You look tired, doll." He leans forward and I close my eyes. Then open them again to find him paused, halfway to my face, like he's debating whether to actually kiss me or not.

"Come on," I urge. "It's just a kiss."

The lips twitch again. He kisses me, just once. Sensual but still perfunctory. Like he's teaching me a lesson I don't understand. Then he releases my face.

"I see you visited my advisor. I told you not to, but thanks."

"I didn't do anything," he maintains and for a moment, I'm taken aback. I didn't read the situation wrong, did I?

And then I realize. It must be standard procedure to never admit a crime out loud.

"Well, thanks for whatever you *didn't* do," I say.

He accepts that with a nod. "I'll sink that fucker in Lake Michigan if he ever disrespects you again."

I give him my widest smile and his eyes crinkle even though his lips don't match mine.

"You hungry? There's this amazing taco joint right

around the corner." I point in the direction of Pancho's Street Tacos.

"You buyin'?"

"Um, yeah," I say, trying to quickly calculate how much cash I have in my wallet.

"Kidding." He swings his door open. "I'll buy. Let's go."

It's ridiculous how excited I feel. Like we're going on a date, rather than me catching him stalking me after brutally attacking my advisor. But I can't find it in me to be afraid of him in this moment. I can't drop the buoyancy that's come over me at seeing him again. Knowing he cared enough about me and my situation to exact his form of justice.

I take him into the taco joint and order my favorite—two grilled shrimp tacos on corn tortillas.

"I'll have the same," he says and gets two drinks to go with them. We take our trays and find a place by the window to squeeze in.

I sit down and take a giant bite. "Mmm, thanks for buying lunch."

He takes a bite of his.

"So why are you still watching me? I thought we were square."

He shrugs. "Making sure you don't leave town suddenly. Or turn yourself in. Or anything else that will make us both sorry."

"Bullshit. You missed me. Admit it."

His lips actually quirk. "A little."

A rush of pleasure rolls through me. "A lot." I finish my first taco and pick up the second.

He neither confirms nor denies.

"Are you still watching my brother?"

He doesn't answer, just takes another mammoth bite of his taco.

"Leave him alone," I warn, all serious now. Not that I have anything to back up my warning. "I mean it. I did what I was supposed to do."

"Then you have nothing to worry about." He finishes his second taco and wipes his mouth with a napkin.

I pick up my lemonade and take a long pull on the straw. "Thanks for lunch," I repeat as I hop off the stool. "I'll see you around, big guy." I give him a saucy wink and a toss of my hair as I sashay out.

It was a great exit and I enjoy getting on my bike and riding away, imagining he's still watching me. It's only after I'm riding that I wonder what would've happened if I'd stayed.

Whether I should've given him my number and told him to call next time instead of watching from his car window.

And then all those thoughts disappear.

Because when I get to my apartment, I find it swarming with FBI.

I guess the jig is up.

## CHAPTER 8

## Caitlin

I GIVE them my full display of fuck-nuts. Every agent who questions me leaves rolling his or her eyes.

And then after a night in jail, and the realization that this may be the rest of my life, I shut down completely.

No more talking. No cray-cray. Nothing.

They'd get more out of a catatonic schizophrenic than they'll get out of shut-down Caitlin.

So when I'm called out of my cell to meet with my lawyer, I barely register it. I hardly see the tall blonde with the firm handshake. I don't hear what she's telling me as she pushes some papers across the desk.

"Ms. West? Do you understand the charges against you?"

I can't bring myself to answer.

She frowns. "You do understand that I'm working for you, right? Are you afraid of Mr. Tacone?"

I blink once. Twice. What is she saying about Mr. Tacone?

"What?"

"Is that why you won't cooperate with me?"

I straighten in my chair and attempt to finger comb my mess of hair out of my face. I glance down at the papers she put in front of me. *Lucy Lawrence.* That's the name of my attorney. "What's happening?"

She cocks her head and gives me the "are you nuts?" expression I'm so used to. "Mr. Tacone hired me to get you out of here. Are you willing to enter into the plea bargain I described?"

I clear my throat. "I'm sorry, would you mind repeating it?"

She's patient with me. Now that I focus, I see she's extraordinarily beautiful and the perfect mix of a sharp professional with the human kindness that's often missing from her type. "You enter a guilty plea in exchange for returning the full amount and we emphasize the fact that you're a graduate student in computer science and this was just an experiment on your part. You didn't believe it would actually work."

I blink some more. "I-I don't have the money to return. It's"—I clear my throat—"gone."

"Mr. Tacone will pony up the missing funds." She gives me a sharp look. "And I have no information about that arrangement."

The world starts to take shape around me again. I'm in a room. With a lawyer Paolo hired to get me out of here.

"Yeah. Okay. Where do I sign?"

"Are you sure?"

"I'm sure." I'll definitely make a deal with the devil to stay out of jail. I was already dead in there. I take the pen from her and sign.

Four hours later they walk me out of my cell, return my personal effects and release me.

I blink in the sunlit room. I'm still moving slowly, as if through molasses, or maybe it just feels that way. I'm in a bubble. There are people all around, but I don't see any I recognize. I pull on my jacket and clutch my bag and step out the door and into the sun.

And fall straight into Paolo Tacone's arms.

∽

*Paolo*

I HOLD CAITLIN, but she's dead weight. There's no life in her face, in her posture, in anything about her. That flame that's usually so bright in her is completely out.

If I could go back in time and make a different arrangement with Caitlin West, I would. How I thought I could watch her go down for the crime she committed because I held her brother's balls in a vise, I can't imagine.

Nothing ever felt so wrong as when I watched her arrest televised on the news. That photo of her flashed on the screen, the picture of her in handcuffs being led away.

I'm pissed as hell it took so long for my lawyer to get her out.

I will seriously commit murder if I find out she was mistreated in there.

"Come on, doll. Let's get you out of here," I tell her.

She lets me maneuver her into the car. She docile. Easy to manage. Possibly in shock.

Is this what shock looks like?

"You okay? Talk to me." I say when I speed away and she still says nothing.

"Where are we going?" she asks dully.

*Cristo,* I would do anything to make her feel better right now. "Where do you want to go?"

"Your place." Her tone is flat, but I'm relieved by the answer. At least she didn't ask me to drop her at home. I'm definitely not willing to leave her alone in this state.

"What do you need, doll? You hungry?"

She turns to look at me, but I don't get the feeling she's seeing anything. After a long moment, she says, "I want you to hurt me."

The flush that runs through me is both lust and fear. My body responds to her request, but my brain rebels. Hurting her is the last thing I want to do right now. And it scares me that she thinks she needs it. But yeah, I'm not going to deny her anything. I'd give my left nut right now if it brought her back to life.

"It helps me come back into my body," she explains.

I relax a little. Okay. She's been here before. This is part of *Cirque du Caitlin*. Fine. I can definitely roll with it.

I take her to my house and bring her to the bathroom where I strip off her clothes and put her in the shower. "How do you want it?" I lean my head through the shower door. I figure I have to prepare while she's cleaning up.

The water runs down her face, over her pale breasts and belly, down her slender legs. "Belt, please. And, Paolo?"

"Yeah, doll?"

"Don't stop until I cry."

My stomach drops. I may like to put the hurt on, but it's contingent on her enjoying herself. Making her cry is something else altogether.

Obviously not a foreign act for me, but it is with a lover.

With someone I care about.

I don't make any promises, I just shake my head. "You're not in charge, are you, little girl?"

I see the first hint of a smile. "Talk tough to me, big guy."

I relax. That's the girl I know. And this is definitely a role I can play for her. And for me. For both of us.

I wait until she's out of the shower and toweled off and then I tie her face down to the bed, arms and legs spread wide. I pick a wide, flexible belt and roll the buckle end around my fist.

"Ready, doll?"

"Mmm," she agrees. She's limp and relaxed—which might be a good thing except I would expect her to have a little more excitement. This isn't post-orgasmic bliss, this is something else.

Not in her body, I guess she said.

I give her a few light spanks with the belt and she doesn't even flinch, so I lay one down hard.

She jerks, buttocks clenching, feet kicking at the ropes I used to secure her.

That has to be a good sign. She felt something, anyway.

I give another hard lick, then another.

The muscles in her back tense and she lifts her head. Her feet jerk in the ropes some more.

"Okay, doll?"

"It's good," she pants. "Really good."

I whip her again and again, keeping it hard enough to produce welts, to make her gasp. Then, after a dozen or so at that pace, I lighten the strokes and go faster. She wiggles and writhes under the belt, moaning.

Still no sign of tears.

*Cazzo,* how much does it take to bring a masochist to tears? Her ass is already red.

I lay a few down on the backs of her thighs, which makes her jump and gasp, then go back to the lighter strokes all over her ass.

I stop and squeeze her cheeks, massaging and kneading them. I dip my fingers between her legs and taste her juices.

Fuck it.

She can take a sex break.

I pull her ass cheeks apart and lick her from clit to anus and back again. The position isn't great, but I flick my tongue over her piercing and tease her folds as much as I can.

"You're going to get fucked hard now, little girl," I warn her.

She turns her face to the side to look at me. Her eyes are soft, like I just said the most romantic thing. "Paolo." There's gratitude in the way she says my name.

I almost laugh. Whips and chains are this girl's roses and chocolate. And that's just fine by me.

I shuck my clothes and roll on a condom. I keep her bound and helpless for the fucking, just climb up over her and slide in.

She clenches around me, that tight pussy squeezing like a fist.

I growl with pleasure and slam in deep. Her body lurches forward, but she only travels an inch, bound too tightly by the ropes.

Perfect.

I brace my weight on my hands and ride her. I close my eyes, savoring the sensation of being inside her again. Of hearing the little moans she makes, the cries.

But then she goes quiet again.

Not wanting to untie her yet, I pull out and get the lube. Anal penetration will be hard to ignore.

I lube us both up generously and push in. I was right, she's back to gasping and crying out, making those cute little sounds of pain and pleasure that get me harder than stone.

I fuck her, working one hand beneath her to rub her clit at the same time.

Her breath turns to pants, her cries grow louder. "Please, Paolo," she begs.

"Come, little hacker," I command, thrusting the cone of my fingers into her pussy as I shove deep into her ass and orgasm.

Her muscles flutter around my fingers and she comes with a strangled cry, her anus tightening almost painfully around my cock.

I wait until she's done to ease out and bring a washcloth to clean her up. I don't untie her, though. Maybe after her orgasm, she'll cry.

I grab a wooden spatula from my kitchen and sit beside her. Last time she cried it was talking about her dad. I don't have it in me to do that to her. Not that I'd even know what to say. I'm about as far from Dr. Phil as they come. I speak more with my actions.

"Look at me, little hacker."

She turns her head, those beautiful blue eyes more open and aware than before, but still lacking her usual fire.

"It's time to give me your tears. You owe me them," I tell her, which may or may not be true, but I know she likes it when I get bossy. I slap her ass with the wooden spatula and she flinches, but then sort of relaxes into bliss.

Harder, then.

I smack the same place with more force and she sucks in her breath on a gasp.

"Ow." First time I've gotten an *ow*. "Thank you, sir."

I smack her just as hard on the other side. "I don't want your thanks. I want your tears. Cry for me, Caitlin." I proceed to paddle her ass, alternating right and left, watching closely as she tenses and holds her breath. Then starts to whimper and jerk.

Still, it's taking too long. I don't want to keep hurting her. She doesn't deserve it, not that this has anything to do with deserve.

"Cry for me, Caitlin. You better cry now or I'll take you back to that jail where I found you today." It's a cruel thing to say but it works. Caitlin breaks.

One sob erupts, then another. I work quickly to untie

her and settle beside her, drawing her into my arms. She burrows into me, crying against my chest until she's wrung out. I stroke her hair, kissing the top of her head.

Hoping to God this is what she needed, and I didn't just cause more harm.

∼

*Caitlin*

Paolo Tacone just saved me from hell.

The man just got me out of jail, then gave me exactly what I needed to shake off the trauma. I rest my head on his chest, blinking at nothing.

All the terror and shame emptied out with my tears. I'm in a state of nothingness now. Drained, but okay. Paolo's on his back and I'm tucked against him, my head resting on his shoulder.

Paolo nudges my face up to peer at me. "You still seem pretty checked out, doll. Did something happen in jail?"

I sense the violence ripple through him, like he's going to slit some throats if he finds out I got jail-raped or something.

"No," I assure him. "I was just scared."

"Understandable."

I lean up on my arm to look at him fully. "Why did you come and get me?" I'm not stupid enough to think I won't owe him big time for this. Favors don't come for free, especially not from mafia men. But I still want to know why he even bothered. I didn't ask for help. He just showed up with it.

Maybe he wants me to start hacking for him on the regular. Some new mafia scheme.

His brow wrinkles. "Girl like you doesn't belong in jail."

I cock my head. "Girl like me?"

"You're like a wildfire—hot. Bright. A fast burn. Nobody should dim your light, doll. I never should have let that happen."

Butterflies take flight in my tummy. He does care. He definitely cares.

"I had a plan going in, you know? I was going to scare you into restoring the money and then let you go. But then I met you. And you're *you*. And I shoulda changed the plan." He shakes his head, regret etched in every line of his face. "I don't know why I didn't." He brushes the backs of his fingers across my collarbone. It's not a sexual touch, but it's intimate. Sensual. "You know I didn't mean what I just said about bringing you back, right?"

"Of course," I answer. And I do. I know he just said the thing that would get me to cry, and that's why I'm floating on gratitude over here. Because there are very few people in this universe who would go there.

But Paolo's an out-of-the-box kind of guy.

I guess you have to be to be a hitman and a sadist to get me.

I don't know why I think that's such a problem.

I straddle his hips, no longer feeling vacant or devoid of emotion. I feel like me again. All parts of me—the complete me. The crazy me. The smart me. The nymphomaniac. The scared me. And still very much grateful me.

I rub my breasts over his chest, purring. "Thank you for rescuing me."

His cock bobs behind me, nudging between my cheeks. He's ready to go again. I rise up and impale myself on his cock slowly, watching his jaw go slack, feeling his length get harder and thicker.

I rock my hips, seating him deeper, and lean forward on my hands, rubbing my boobs over his hairy bear-chest. "So what is your plan for me now, big man?"

He grips my hips and starts conducting, pulling me over him to ride his cock. Controlling the show.

"This was pretty much my plan." His voice is gravelly. I like the way his breath stutters out on the exhale.

"You're going to keep me as your love-slave?" I purr.

Of course the idea turns me on—I'm a little maso who loves to be used. But that's just thinking about it as a short-term kinky scene. In actuality, this could be my worst nightmare. Still, I can't muster the reservations I should be feeling right now.

"Uh huh. No disrespect intended, of course. That gonna work for you?"

I sit back on my haunches and let him bounce me over his cock, my tits swinging. "For how long?"

"I figure you can work off your debt to me, one sex act at a time. Just like this."

Okay. So still a prisoner. Just a longer timeline now. Good to know.

I run my nails through the hair on his chest. Scrape them lightly across his nipples. "What's the going rate?"

He thrusts his hips up while pulling me down, forcing me to take him deep. "Let's say five hundred bucks per sex act. And I'll even count all the times you got me off last week, since that was so generous of you. Especially considering I was shaking you down."

My mouth stretches into a wide smile.

He doesn't return the expression, but he says, "I like it when you smile like that. You're really fucking hot, Caitlin."

And then I want desperately to please him. I reach behind and cup his balls, rub over his prostate while I ride him.

Paolo growls and flips us over, so I'm on the bottom and he's on the top. He leans on one hand and strokes in and out, staring down at my face like I'm the most fascinating thing he's ever seen.

I pinch his nipples. He pins my hands beside my head. "I'm not wearing a condom."

"I'm on the pill," I say automatically. Of course I missed a couple nights when he kidnapped me but I made them up and I can make up last night's missed pill, too.

"Good, because I want to come inside you." He doesn't worry about my orgasm this time, which I find kinda hot. Like I'm his love slave now so my pleasure isn't his concern. Basically, it just ensures that I come as hard as he does, maybe harder.

And then he grins. It transforms the normally gruff expression on his face.

He makes no comment, just sends this affectionate smile as he hovers over me, still buried deep.

WILD CARD

We stare at each other like neither of is sure how we got here, but we're glad we did.

And for just this moment, I want to forget everything—grad school, jail, my father's death, foster care, taking care of my brother. I want to forget Paolo Tacone is a powerful hitman for the mob and just *be*.

Just be with him.

Too bad life is so damn complicated.

∽

*Paolo*

CAITLIN LOSES her smile as soon as we're out of bed. She picks up her phone and goes outside—buck naked and it's forty degrees out—to make a phone call. I watch her through the sliding door, circling the hot tub. When she opens it up to peek inside, I step outside to pull the cover back. "Hop in," I murmur, smacking her ass.

She tosses me a grateful smile and scoots in, but the tone of the conversation she's having is tense. "Listen, it's all been handled. You don't need to worry about it, okay? No, the charges were dropped, the money was returned. All's well that ends well."

I go inside to give her some privacy. It's probably her brother. When I scrolled through her phone the first night, that was the only number she called for more than a minute.

I vow to learn more about her life—family, history,

everything. Now that I've decided to keep my little wildfire, I want to know everything there is to know.

I bring out a towel and leave it for her. When she comes back in, she's a more sane Caitlin—a side I haven't seen much of, but I knew must be there for her to be where she is—halfway to a PhD in computer science. "I was supposed to TA my first class today," she says, like all is lost.

There's no fucking way this is a problem, though. Not when Dr. Alden is my bitch now.

I point at her phone. "Call your advisor. Tell him you'll be there tomorrow."

"Well, it would be next Tuesday, but..." She searches my face. "Okay." She dials and I step closer to listen in. She's wrapped in nothing but a towel, and even though I've already had her twice, she still turns me on.

She glances up at me again, as if for reassurance as she puts the phone to her ear. "Hi, Dr. Alden? Yeah, I don't know if you saw the news or not, but—"

"I saw it," he says tightly. "Are you calling from jail?"

"Nope, I'm out. Charges have been dropped. It was all a big misunderstanding." She shoots me another look and I nod reassuringly. "So I missed today's class, but I'll start Tuesday, no problem."

"No problem, right," he grumbles, but then he says, "Fine. Make sure you do."

"I'll make sure," she says.

I resist the urge to snatch the phone from her hand and tell him he'd better sweeten his fucking tone when he talks to my girl, but I leave it.

Caitlin hangs up and falls into me, pressing her body

against mine. I wrap an arm around her. But her forehead wrinkles up again. "Um, I need to go home." She sends me a pleading look. "I'm way behind in my schoolwork and—"

I hold up my hand. "Say no more. You're not my prisoner, doll. I'll drive you back."

I'm annoyed by her relief, even though how the fuck is she supposed to know she's not a prisoner this time? I'm the kind of guy who purposely keeps people in the dark about where they stand and what my intentions are.

I've spent my entire life hiding what's important to me behind violence and threats. I don't even know how to let another person in. My family, they just know me. Communication isn't required.

But a prickly sensation tells me I'm going to fall way off the mark with Caitlin if I don't figure this shit out.

Trouble is, I don't even know where to start.

*~*

*Caitlin*

I DON'T HEAR from Paolo for a couple days, which comes as a relief because I have a lot of catching up and explaining to do with my classes and job at the rec center.

That doesn't mean I'm not thinking about him every second of the day. Wondering when he's going to turn up.

If he'll be sitting in my living room when I come home. Or if he's watching me. I had this sense before the FBI picked me up that I was being watched. At the time I imagined it was them, but after the thing with Dr. Alden I've started wondering if it was Paolo.

And all this time, I hear the scream of warning going off about this whole situation. I literally got into bed with a killer. I owe him two hundred grand which I am paying off one blowjob at a time.

Things could go south in an instant.

On the third night I come home from my dance cardio class and find my apartment has been completely emptied.

I stand in the doorway, my heart thumping as I try to figure out what happened.

Is this a message from Paolo? Did he feel like I didn't make myself available so he took all my belongings? Or did the FBI return? No, that doesn't make sense.

"Oh hey, doll." Paolo appears behind me, his large hand spanning my lower back. "I moved your shit. Come on."

"Moved it where?" I say faintly. He takes my bike from my hands and carries it down the stairwell in front of me.

Outside, he hands the bike to some young Italian guy with a shining red Escalade on the corner. "Bring that over, too," he says to the guy.

"What's happening, Paolo?"

We get to his car and he opens the passenger door for me. "Get in."

I wring my hands in the car. Did he move me into his place? It's way too far from campus, and I don't drive. Living there would be the biggest pain in my ass. Plus... I'm scared. I don't know what it means to be consumed by Paolo Tacone.

The drive isn't far, though. Just a mile away, he pulls into a newly remodeled upscale apartment building where I'm sure the apartments cost five times what mine does.

"What's going on?" I ask Paolo again, but he still refuses to answer. The guy with my bike shows up right behind us, and Paolo takes it from him and hands him a wad of cash. "*Grazie*, Adam."

Seriously, I could've ridden my bike over here and he could've given me that cash.

"Come on, little hacker." Paolo carries my bike in and we get on the elevator to the sixth floor. There, he unlocks the door to an apartment.

It's lovely. Gleaming hardwood floors. Bay windows on the street side of the apartment. A leather couch with dual recliners and a matching chair face a giant flat-screen television. There's a nice rug in front of it.

My desk and bulletin board are against one wall, with my computer equipment all set up.

"What's happening?" I try again.

"I moved you. I didn't like that other place. It was a dump and not nearly safe enough for you." He walks over and sprawls on the expensive couch. "What do you think?"

Great. I try to erase the frown from my face. Yeah, he does have the right to move me. This guy owns me.

So I should show some gratitude. Credit another $500 off my tab.

I walk over and hit my knees in front of him, reaching for his cock.

He catches my wrist. "Hang on, little girl."

I look up, checking his face for clues about what he wants. What I did wrong.

"It's not that I don't want you to give me head." He leans forward and brushes some of my hair back from my face. "I always want that, doll. But I get the feeling you didn't like my surprise. What gives?"

I suck my cheek into my mouth and consider what to say. "It's definitely a surprise," I say cautiously. "But the thing is, I could never afford a place like this on my own. So I give up my cheap student housing—and I had to use some serious hacking skills to make sure I won that lottery when it came open—and then what happens when we're done?"

Paolo goes perfectly still. He never shows much, but I can tell whatever I said upset him. "What do you mean *when we're done*?"

And that's when it hits me—Paolo Tacone might be playing for keeps.

And I'm not sure why that scares me even more than our current arrangement.

He cups my chin and lifts it to examine my face. "Let me ask you something… are you keeping track?"

*Keeping track.* He means of how much I owe him.

I nod, even though I'm pretty sure it's going to piss him off.

It does. He releases me abruptly and gets up, stepping over me to pace to the window. In the reflection, I watch him scrub a hand over his five o'clock shadow and stare down at the cars below.

Crap.

I am in over my head here. I don't know what's going through his mind, or if I even want to know.

But I do get that I just hurt his feelings.

A feat I didn't believe possible until this moment.

I walk over and touch his arm.

He jerks it up and I flinch, but he was only moving to loop his arm around me. I relax and let him and he draws me close. "You're scared of me." He sounds stunned. Like he hadn't considered that possibility. I guess I've done a good job hiding it. My overly-familiar act sucked him right in.

I can't answer, because I don't want to acknowledge what's obviously an offensive notion to him.

He releases me and gives a shake of his head. "You want out of our arrangement?"

My breath stands still. It's a simple question. And considering I have been keeping track, you'd think it would be an easy answer. But when I open my mouth, nothing comes out.

"No," I finally croak.

He lifts his brows like he doesn't believe me. "No? I can find another way for you to pay me back. A couple years working IT at the casino when you graduate. You don't even have to see me again. Would you prefer that?"

Why is my heart breaking at this questioning? I should be jumping at the offer. It's far safer. Much more reasonable.

Instead I wrap my arms around his thick trunk. "I don't want out of the arrangement. But I am scared."

He burrows his fingers into the back of my hair and cradles my head. He tips my face up and leans his forehead against mine. "But you like to be afraid, right, little hacker?"

A soft puff of laughter leaves my lips. Once again, I'm surprised at how easily he sees my quirks. "You got me."

His thumb moves behind my neck, stroking there. "I thought we understood each other." His dark gaze sears my face. "Was I wrong?"

I shake my head. Because my anxieties have fled. It's illogical and unreal, but in these moments, I do believe I understand Paolo Tacone perfectly. And I believe he understands me.

It's when I'm away from him I realize none of this is safe, sane or consensual. None of this makes sense.

He runs his thumb over my lower lip, then tilts my head and drops his to brush his lips across mine. "Let's get this straight once and for all. I play rough. I like to say I own you. Order you around and remind you what you owe me. But all of that makes you hot. Am I wrong?"

"No."

"You like being owned by me."

I hesitate.

His eyes narrow as he studies me. "What am I missing?"

"Nothing. No, you're right. But what I think is hot and what I think is smart or safe, aren't necessarily the same things."

He cups my nape. "Baby, I never hurt you."

"You kidnapped me and held my brother for ransom."

He drops his head to the side. "Well, you had it coming. You stole from me."

A giggle escapes my lips. This man is possibly as nuts as I am. "True." I put my hands on his chest and step closer. "So what are we really talking about? This is more than a business arrangement?"

He releases me and rubs his forehead. "Do you want it to be?"

I cast my gaze about the room as if the answer to this might appear somewhere on the freshly painted walls. "I-I don't know. I mean, I don't even know what I'd bring to something more than that. I'm just a crazy hacker who gives good head."

"I know you're not crazy." He considers me. "What do I bring to the table besides some money and a mean streak?" He shrugs. "Maybe I need somebody to hurt. Someone to submit. You like pain. And yeah, you give great fucking head. It's a match made in heaven."

I laugh and hold his gaze as I lower to my knees. His nostrils flare when I unbuckle his belt. His cock grows as soon as I touch it, lengthening and bobbing when it springs free from his boxers. I take a slow, leisurely lick around the head.

"Caitlin, this isn't a transaction for me." His voice is strained—whether it's from the blowjob or the difficulty in admitting anything to me, I can't tell.

I take him deep into my mouth as an answer.

But he persists. "Is it for you?"

I grip the base of his cock and squeeze tight, coming off with my mouth. I shake my head. "I missed you after the kidnapping."

His lips quirk and he grips the back of my head, feeding his length into my mouth again. "I missed you, too, *bella*."

I struggle against his hold until he sets me free and I

pop back off. "So am I your girlfriend? Are you going to see other women at the same time?"

He raises his brows, and the amusement on his face pisses me off. "Would that bother you?"

I stand up. Blow job is officially over. "I don't play side chick," I snap, turning away.

He catches my arm and yanks me into a brutal kiss. His tongue presses between my lips, teeth nip at me. When he releases me and comes up for air, he says, "No one else. Tacones don't do side chicks. Once we make our minds up about a woman, we're loyal as hell."

I absorb that nugget, fascinated by everything it brings up. He comes from a family of violent but loyal men. That's hot in a raw, primeval way.

To my utter shock, he drops to his knees and yanks down my yoga pants. His tongue delves between my legs and I cry out, grasping his hair. He rubs and flicks his tongue over all my sensitive bits until I'm trying to climb onto his face.

"Clothes off," he orders when I start pulling his hair. "Go check out your new bed."

I giggle and kick off my shoes and pants and run for the bedroom. It's another lovely, large room with a huge four poster king bed in the middle. I grab one of the posts and swing around to face him where he's stalking up behind me like the predator he is. "Are these for tying me up?"

"You know it." He slaps my bare ass. "Why do you still have clothes on?"

I scramble out of my sweater, crop top and sports bra and climb up on the bed. "On your back. Spread your legs." For a moment, he just takes his fill of looking, his dark eyes glittering with promise. Then he produces several lengths of soft rope from his pocket—he must have planned my bondage in advance—and ties me spread-eagle to the posts. Pleasure courses through my veins before he even touches me and when he returns to his exploration of my pussy with this tongue, I'm already half-lost.

Three orgasms later, I'm shaking and begging him to stop.

"No more. Please, Paolo. I can't take any more. Let me suck your cock."

He gives a cruel laugh. "Next time I'll tie you with your head facing the foot of the bed and then fuck your mouth. You'd like that, wouldn't you, little slave?"

"Mmm hmm." I'm delirious at this point. But he's right, I'd love that.

He unties me and climbs over me. I wrap my legs around his back when he enters me and use my heels to pull him in deeper.

He rocks into me, and even though I'm already wrung out with all the orgasms, my body shivers and celebrates the penetration.

"I like the apartment," I confess. I attempt to focus on my surroundings. "I like the bed, too." He rolls my knees back toward my shoulders and pumps into me rapid-fire. Then he switches to put my ankles over his shoulders. Finally, he turns me onto my belly and finishes fucking me from behind.

"I can't move," I groan after he comes, because my body is as limp as a rag doll.

Paolo sits down on the bed and pulls me face down over his lap. He spanks me hard and fast, which instantly wakes me up. "Ow!" I reach back with my hand to cover my butt.

He grabs my wrist and bends it behind my back, continuing to spank me. "I've seen you take way worse."

"Not after so many orgasms!" I protest. "I'm way more sensitive now."

"Is that right? Didn't know that."

"Yes! It's a fact." I try to cover with the other hand, squeezing my buttocks together and kicking my feet with straight legs like a swimmer. "What'd I do, anyway?"

"You don't have to do anything to get spanked, little girl. Sometimes I just feel like doling out the pain."

I smile. Because despite my protests, this is total bliss for me. He's definitely a man who speaks my language. "Good thing that works for me."

"Good thing."

This man is every masochist's dream, but there's no way I'm going to point him to the BDSM scene to discover there's a whole slew of submissives like me who would gladly offer up their bodies to this perfect, wealthy dominant.

"I can't believe some girl hasn't latched on to you to be her sugar daddy before."

He pops me twice on the ass—one spank on each cheek. "Is that what I am now?"

I giggle. "Well, you did just get me a new apartment."

He wraps his hand in my hair and uses it to bow my back up and lift my face. "I'm happy to spoil the shit out of you, doll, if that's what you like."

I get wet, even though I'm not the type who goes crazy over money. I've made do on very little since I was emancipated at the age of sixteen. But we just said this isn't transactional.

"I'm just here for the sex," I say with a saucy smile. "And because you own me."

He slaps the backs of my thighs, which makes me kick in earnest. "I do own you. And I'm going to take every advantage of that." He drags his thumb between my butt cheeks and I squeeze even harder.

"What happens if we break up?"

"What?" He tugs me up to straddle his lap and pushes the hair back from my face.

"With the money? The arrangement? What happens then?"

"Then we make a new arrangement."

I still have all kinds of yellow flags, if not red. My better judgement still thinks I should be running for the hills right now. "Have you ever hit a woman?" I have to know if this guy would get violent with me. Like if he got jealous, or we had a fight.

"What?" His brows slam down, nostrils flare.

I've really offended him.

"Never." He shakes his head emphatically. "I would never hit a woman. Not for any reason, other than the one you already know." He squeezes my ass to make it clear which one that is.

I suck in a breath. Crazy Caitlin wants to get this all settled and out in the open. "Have you ever killed a woman?"

"No. But I don't answer questions like that, Caitlin.

Don't ask me about anything illegal ever again. I won't answer—for your own protection. *Capiche*?"

A shiver runs down my spine, but far from scaring me off, I'm just more turned on. My nipples pebble up. I don't even know why that turns me on. He's dangerous, but he has this code he lives by. He doesn't hurt women. He doesn't talk about what he's done.

It's far different from the way my dad would endlessly brag about the small-time operations he was a part of.

I initiate the kiss this time and he lets me lead, fingers tightening on my back.

"I'm sorry I offended you earlier," I say.

He shakes his head. "I wasn't offended." But I know it's not true. And now that I've seen a little sliver of the man beneath the tough guy, I feel more comfortable with our arrangement.

Relationship.

With being his girlfriend.

I'm still nervous. I still have reservations, the main one still revolving around my father's death. Like—did one of his brothers do it? One of their soldiers? He's already told me he won't tell if he finds out. Can I really open my heart to an actual relationship with a man whose family is responsible for the wrecking of mine?

It's a hard hump to get over.

But I can try.

CHAPTER 9

*Paolo*

"Take that!" Caitlin jumps up and down on the bed naked, throwing pillows at me. When she runs out of missiles, I tackle her to the mattress and spank her ass.

It's been two weeks since we entered our arrangement. I'm not the kinda guy who's ever really considered happiness, but I think I've found it. I split my time between Caitlin's apartment and my house, trying to leave her enough time to study and teach her classes and, of course, work out, because those are the things she enjoys.

And the rest of the time I do my best to spoil her with food, sex, experiences. I keep her wallet loaded with money, not that she ever spends much.

"It's the weekend, what should we do?" I ask, biting her shoulder. "Do you have a lot of work?"

"I always have work, but let's do something. Let's—" She gasps. "I know!"

I roll her over so I can see her face. "What?"

Uncertainty flickers there. "Um, do you want to go to Vegas?"

I slide my fingers between her wet folds. "Do you?"

She squeezes her thighs around my hand. "Well," she says breathlessly. "I've never been. And I heard there's this really great casino there."

"Yeah, but I heard they have shitty cybersecurity." I raise my brows.

She wriggles her hips when I sink a finger in her wet heat. "Oh, I think it's been beefed way up. But um… do you think they'll let me in?"

I scoff. "It's my place, doll. Nobody's going to throw you out. Let's go."

"Really?" She scrambles off the bed and out of my reach, already dashing for the closet to pull out a ridiculous purple suitcase. "I've never been before. I've always wanted to go. I'm so excited!"

I smile. The warmth in my chest is a new feeling. All of this is. Her excitement. Her receptivity. Her laughter. I've never had anything like this before and it feels damn good. I get to see all parts of Caitlin now—the crazy, the fun, the serious, the hard-working. And I'm charmed by all of them.

The safer she feels with me, the more her crazy softens into child-like enthusiasm and joy.

I sit and watch her pack as she bombards me with questions about what she'll need. "Swim suit?"

I nod. "Three pools. All warm."

"Fancy clothes? Sexy clothes?"

"Anything goes. What would be fun for you, little hacker?"

"How about this?" She holds up a bright red dress with swaths of see-through red fabric across the belly and neckline and arms.

"Perfect. Sexy always flies in Vegas."

I get on my phone and find us the next first-class flight out of Chicago.

∿

Two hours later, we're in the air.

Caitlin's practically bouncing in her seat, her fingers twined with mine. She leans over and flicks her tongue in my ear. "Have you joined the mile high club?"

"Do you want to?"

She nods. I'm not about to tell her I already have—with some stripper on a party jet once—not when she's so excited. I glance around us, then at the bathrooms.

"I'll tell you what. I'll book a private jet for the flight home. We will never both fit in those bathrooms and I'm not about to let anyone see you doing anything out here."

"A private jet? Are you serious?"

I pinch her chin and pull her face forward for a kiss. "If you're a good girl."

"I'll be good," she purrs. "Or a bad girl. Whatever you want."

"I want you every way," I tell her.

*Caitlin*

I've never been on vacation, except for the summer trips to our grandparents' cabin. Trevor and I used to spend all day up there boating around on the lake, playing in the forest, catching frogs and fish.

When my dad died, the cabin passed on to us, but we haven't been there much. It's hard when neither of us has a driver's license to get there.

But Vegas is everything I imagined. Bright lights, people everywhere. Something interesting to look at in every direction.

The Bellissimo is incredible. A porter dashes out to open the door to the limo when we arrive. He takes my hand and helps me out of the car.

"Welcome, Mr. Tacone," he says, inclining his head when Paolo gets out. "I'll get your bags right up to your suite." He hands him a room key envelope.

Paolo takes the key and puts his hand on my lower back, guiding me into the lobby. The Bellissimo itself is smaller than many of the other casinos on the strip—more of a boutique, which is what makes it so popular. It's plush and posh on the inside, with Italian marble everywhere, and a rainbow bridge of real flowers. My eyes are probably as wide as saucers as we go in.

It occurs to me I should act like a grownup—like I'm not so impressed and I travel all the time. But with Paolo, I don't have to. I can be Crazy Caitlin, and he thinks I'm cute without underestimating me.

So I let her out to run and explore.

Our room is way at the top—on the 26th floor and it's bigger than my entire apartment. It's a suite with a living room and a kitchen and the most luxurious bathroom I've ever seen. There's a giant jacuzzi tub and a walk-in shower with two showerheads.

"Last one in the shower is a rotten egg!" I shout, stripping my clothes off.

Paolo joins me, not rushing, not slow. Just his usual steady, solid, imposing way. He fills the giant shower stall and it immediately seems more like a normal size.

I drop to my knees and give him my best thank you blow job. He grips my head, but his touch is gentle; he's massaging my scalp as he pulls me over his cock. "Caitlin…"

I try to look up through the spray of water and he moves his back to block it from hitting my face.

"You're beautiful, doll. You give the best head." He's already losing control. "You gonna swallow me down like a good girl?"

I nod and massage his balls, which are tightened up, ready to release. He comes and pulls me up to stand. Kisses me so hard I lose my breath. It's a violent, claiming kiss and it makes my knees go weak. When he releases my face and strokes my clit, I shiver, teetering on the edge of an orgasm.

"Don't come," he murmurs.

I pout. "Orgasm denial is mean."

His brows lift. "That a thing? Of course that's a thing."

Damn! I am an idiot for telling him.

"You're definitely going to have to wait, then." He removes his fingers from my pussy and I nearly weep.

"No, no, no, no," I beg. "Don't make me wait. I'll go crazy."

I see the sadist in his grin. "Good." He gives me a slap on the ass. "Now go get ready, so I can show you around."

I climb out of the shower and wrap one of the posh bathrobes around me to head to the bedroom. My body's on fire from the edging and I jump up and down to let some energy off.

Maybe this is all I need to do to make sure I never disassociate again. Just edge myself in the morning with a vibe as a preventative measure. I grin at the idea.

A knock sounds on the door. Paolo's still in the shower, so I go answer the door.

A younger version of Paolo stands there. He's shockingly handsome, and his aura is smooth, debonair and sophisticated where Paolo's is rugged and tough.

His brows shoot up when he sees me. "*Oh.* I didn't know Paolo had a guest."

Oh crap. And I'm the girl who stole a hundred fifty grand from his family. I hope he's as forgiving as Paolo.

I stick out my hand, still damp from the water. "Hi, I'm Caitlin." I sound overly bright. Crazy Caitlin is showing and I don't want her to. I want to be normal. Likeable.

In the bathroom, the shower turns off. I pray Paolo will get out here and fix this before I get thrown in Lake Mead.

"Wait... Caitlin *West*?" his voice drips disbelief. Or shock.

Shit.

Paolo said I wouldn't get kicked out, but I'm not sure his brother's on the same page.

"One fucking word and I'll smash your face in," Paolo growls from the bedroom door. He's wearing nothing but a towel wrapped around his waist and it couldn't be more obvious that we just showered together.

His brother flicks his gaze from Paolo to me and back again, his expression growing interested. He leans against the doorway. "I *see*."

"I'm serious." Paolo stalks forward.

"I'm not gonna say anything," his brother says mildly, holding his hands up in surrender. "But for future reference, a little communication is all it takes, P. Send a quick text—*the hacker is my girl now, treat her with respect*—that's all."

"Fuck you, *stronzo*."

"Yeah, fuck you, too," he says, but his tone is good-natured and the two men clasp hands and shake. "I'd hug you, but it looks like you're a little wet." He stretches his hand out to me. "I'm Stefano. Paolo's brother."

"My baby brother," Paolo says.

"I can tell." I shake his hand.

"Enjoy your time at the Bellissimo." He pulls a Bellissimo poker chip out of his pocket and hands it to me. My eyes bug out when I see it has $500 printed in the middle. Maybe he doesn't hold a grudge.

To Paolo, he says, "I'm guessing you don't have time for a family dinner?"

Paolo shoots a glance at me. "No, that'd be good, actually. I need to talk to you and Nico and Vlad."

A prickle runs down my spine. It's clearly something I

can't hear. Is it about me? No, I'm getting paranoid again. Nothing's going to happen.

Stefano cocks his head like he's surprised, but he pulls out his phone. "I'll text Alessia to set it up. Tonight? Tomorrow?"

"Tomorrow. *Grazie*, Stefano." He says something else in Italian that I don't understand and Stefano shuts the door.

"You okay? Did he offend you?"

I hold up the five hundred dollar token. "I guess we're good."

Paolo's expression turns indulgent. "You can gamble to your little heart's delight, doll. We got you covered."

I want to blow him all over again, but the edging has me zinging, plus I can't wait to get downstairs and see the casino, so I scurry to put on my red dress and dry my hair.

~

Two hours and three signature cocktails later, I'm tipsy as hell and up sixteen hundred dollars. My coding brain is all over the roulette wheel. There are easy rules to winning with it. I bet red—for the lucky dress—every time. If I lose, I double the bet the next time. The only way the method doesn't work is if you run out of money before you make it back. Fortunately, that hasn't happened. I'm not sure Paolo would even let it happen. He stands at my back playing sugar daddy. Protecting me, ordering me drinks, making small rumbles of approval every time.

The cocktail waitress comes by and hands me another drink, but Paolo takes it from my hand.

I turn to run a fingertip over his fine Italian suit jacket. "Am I cut off, big man?" I might be slurring slightly.

"Let's get some food into you first, doll."

"Oh yeah. I guess we skipped dinner." I also might be swaying slightly. It's a good call on his part, because now that he mentions dinner, I realize I'm getting a little nauseous, which is unusual for me.

Paolo asks the croupier to change out my chips and he tucks them in his pocket. "I'll keep them for you, unless you want to hold them?"

"No, you can. I'm rich." I beam at him.

We turn to leave but we're blocked by a tall gorgeous redhead in stilettos. "Paolo, good to see you." She leans in and they exchange cheek kisses on both sides. She's cool and sophisticated. Not overly eager. Definitely confident.

I instantly hate her until Paolo says, "Caitlin, this is Corey, my sister-in-law—Stefano's wife."

I relax into a smile and shake her hand. She looks to be my age—maybe we'll be friends. Even drunk I realize what a crazy thought that is. Am I actually inserting myself into Paolo's life? Like I'm really seeing things long-term with him?

I think I am.

"Oh hi. I met your husband earlier. Nice to meet you."

"Same. Are you having fun? Looks like you know how to play the hell out of the roulette table."

"Corey used to work as a croupier here until Stefano snatched her away. She's also a poker champ," Paolo says.

Corey lifts her brows in surprise and jerks her thumb at him. "I've never heard him so conversational before. Who knew?"

I beam, because she's right, he does conserve words and I have a feeling he's using them now to put me at ease. I stand on tiptoe to give him a kiss on the cheek. "He saves his words up for when I need them." I hope she can't tell how drunk I am.

Corey splits a glance between us and smiles. "I'm glad you came, Caitlin." She seems to really mean it.

"We're going to get some food," Paolo tells her. "See you tomorrow for sure."

As Paolo leads me away I say, "It's a good thing she's married. I thought I was going to have to throat punch her there for a minute."

Paolo stops and pulls me into his arms, amusement and affection dancing on his normally inexpressive face. "I told you, little hacker. I don't cheat."

I blink up at him. I'm swoony but I'm also drunk. I want to hash everything out now. All the crazy thoughts swirling through my brain about why I shouldn't be with him. Right here on the casino floor. In front of everyone. "What if *I* cheat?"

His brows slam down. "Are you fucking kidding me?"

Clearly the wrong thing to ask.

But I want to know. He says he won't hurt me but he's a dangerous man. What happens if I cross a line? What *are* those lines?

"I won't—I don't either," I assure him quickly. I grab his arm. "I promise. It's just—"

"What?" He's still pissed. That shouldn't excite me. I am wired so wrong.

Because I'm tipsy, I lightly slap his chest. "You

kidnapped me and threatened my brother's life! I just need to know what happens if I piss you off."

Anger ripples over Paolo's expression and he steps back and scrubs a hand over this face. Then he shakes his head. "No more of this," he says.

I shake my head. I'm already getting queasy. "You can't tell me *no more*."

Of course he can. He just did. And that's exactly the point I'm testing here. I'm with a dangerous, controlling man.

He throws his hands in the air in that distinctly Italian way. "What do you want from me?"

"What if I ran away?"

"You gonna run?"

"No, but what if I did? What's the line?"

Exasperation dances over his face and he narrows his eyes, but I can tell he's thinking about his answer. "Okay, where's the line?" He catches my chin and lifts it to bring our faces close. "If it's business, I'm gonna deal with you in a business-like fashion. You steal from the casino, you threaten my family, talk to the Feds, we're done and the gloves come off. If it's personal, I'm not a douche. You break my heart, there's no retribution. That plain enough for you?"

He's annoyed with me, but I'm too dizzy over his words.

*You break my heart…*

That implies he has a heart to break. And that he's given it to me.

Can that be possible?

I beam at him. "Yes. Thank you."

He frowns. "Yes? I said the right thing? I'm not sure how that's possible. Little girl, you never swing the way I think you will."

My smile gets wider. "And that's why you love me," I sing.

His lips slowly quirk. "You're lucky you're so fucking cute." He throws me over his shoulder and carries me through the throng of staring strangers until we reach one of the restaurants in the casino. There he sets me down gently and straightens my clothes.

"Table for two, Mr. Tacone?" the hostess chirps.

He nods. When she walks away, he says, "Stop planning for the end, Caitlin." His voice is gruff but I catch a trace of vulnerability in his expression, and I suddenly regret all my doubt.

And he's right. I'm still planning the end because that's all I've known in relationships.

I step into him and nuzzle his neck. I kiss the skin above his collar.

He cradles my head with both hands. "I *really* like you, Caitlin."

I beam at him. "Is that the same as love?"

He doesn't move. I get the feeling he's never said it before.

Neither have I, except to my brother.

He leans down and moves his lips across mine. "I think it is," he murmurs.

Fireworks explode in my chest, my belly, the backs of my knees—everywhere.

He loves me. I don't say it back. Not because it's not

true, only because… I still feel like I have to protect myself.

This man owns me. I give him my body, but I'm not sure about my soul yet. I'm especially not sure about my heart.

He controls so much. Maybe I just need one thing I can still hold back from him.

CHAPTER 10

*Paolo*

We take a limo from the Bellissimo to Alessia and Vlad's mansion in Summerland North, the richest neighborhood in Vegas. I normally prefer to drive myself and would've just taken one of Nico's expensive cars from the private garage, but I want to give Caitlin all the experiences. Spa treatments. Room service. Ziplining between rooftops. Roller coasters. She's loved all of them. She drank too much last night and was queasy this morning, but perked right up after ordering everything on the room service menu.

Everything's new to her and she's not defensive about receiving any of it. She doesn't try to pretend it's not exciting, or that she doesn't want it. She greets it all with this crazy, childish enthusiasm that keeps my dick hard and my chest warm.

After dinner last night, we saw one of our soldiers, Tony, escorting his girl Pepper Heart backstage before her performance. Caitlin went nuts when she saw the singer, and was over the moon when I called out to Tony for an introduction. She snapped at least a dozen selfies with Pepper, who was as sweet as pie about it.

I meant it when I said I loved her last night. I didn't even feel vulnerable saying it, even though she didn't say it back.

I don't ever feel weak with her.

I know we have a long way to go. I'm not stupid enough to think good sex is enough to make a relationship work, and I also know the newness of money and power will wear off.

Right now, she's gone silent, though. No bouncing or looking out the windows at everything.

"Hey," I say. "What's up?"

She looks at me, but her eyes are blank, like she's far away. She shakes her head. This is a part of her—it's why she believes she's crazy. Why she turns to pain and pleasure to feel alive. What made her go dead?

"You have the same look you had after you spent the night in jail. You nervous about meeting my family?"

She nods, still remote.

I reach over and unbuckle the seatbelt and pull her onto my lap. "What do you need?" I slide my fingers between her legs. She's in a mini-dress with nothing but a scrap of fabric over her pussy. I stroke gently and her head flops back on my shoulder.

"This."

"Yeah?" I bite her ear. "You need pain, too? Or just pleasure?"

"Anything. It helps bring me back into my body."

I want to ask her more. I'm pissed at myself for not finding out everything there is to know about her and her quirks before I expose her to situations that make her tap out.

I slip under the panties and stroke lightly until she gets wet. When she does, I increase the pressure, spreading her juices up to her clit and toying with the piercing.

"You know I'm not gonna let anyone mistreat you, right? These are my younger brothers. They would never fuck with me."

She doesn't answer, but she's rocking her hips over my hardened cock, her pussy weeping for more.

"Caitlin?" I prompt when she doesn't answer. I slip my fingers out of her panties and slap her pussy.

She moans her appreciation.

And then it hits me. Even though I'm going over there today to ask my brothers in person about her dad, it hadn't dawned on me that she's gonna be wondering if they did it.

I spank her pussy again, a dozen light quick slaps. "They didn't kill your dad, Caitlin. They were here in Vegas at the time. *Lo prometo*—I promise."

She whimpers and her back tightens like she's holding in a sob.

Fuck. I'm an insensitive asshole for not realizing that's why she was checking out.

Of course that would be too much for somebody to handle—going to meet her boyfriend's family when they might be the ones who killed her father? Her loyalty between her father and me must be tearing her up inside.

I say more than I ever intended to tell her. "I really don't think it was us, doll. He was working with the Russians, too. I'm gonna follow up there. But it wasn't my brother-in-law, either. He was living in Russia at the time."

She turns and throws her arms around my neck and buries her head against my shoulder. Her entire body trembles. She's holding her breath.

"You can cry if you need to, little girl. Or I can fuck you blind. Whatever the hell you want."

Her tears wet my neck, but she whispers, "I'll take the second option" and peels off her panties.

"On your knees," I command. "Bend over the seat." There's plenty of room for me to pound her from behind, and I figure that's how she wants it.

Judging by how quickly she drops into position, I'd say I guessed right.

I unzip and stand on my knees behind her, holding her torso down, even though she's not resisting.

I rub the head of my cock over her slit and then slide in, the shudder of pleasure immediate. We don't have much time, so I make it count. I hold her by her nape and pump into her.

"Oh God, yes," she moans.

She feels so good, but this isn't for me. I need to make her come. Give her what she needs. I jackhammer into her, make it hard and rough. She arches her back to take me deeper, picks her head up from the seat.

I wrap my hand over her mouth and plug her nose with my thumb.

She jerks in surprise and struggles. I let her breathe again. "I don't wanna leave marks on your neck, *bella*, so you're gonna hold your breath until you come. Understand?"

"Yes, sir."

"Good girl." I keep fucking her hard and block her air passages again. This time she's ready. She doesn't fight it at first. Then she struggles. I let her breathe again.

"This time," I tell her sternly. "This time you're going to come, *capiche*?"

"Okay, yes. Please."

I chuckle at the *please*. So damn cute. I cover her mouth and nose again. I told her how it's going down, and apparently my balls are also on board, because they tighten up, heat flashes at the base of my spine. I close my mouth on a shout and bury myself deep in her to come, pulling her torso up off the seat and back against my chest.

She lets out a cry against my hand and then she comes. Violently. Her body jerks and twitches. Her cunt squeezes and releases.

I don't want it to end. I definitely don't want to get out of the limo. But it's stopped. The driver is being cool because I told him I'd take care of him if he took care of me.

"Are you okay, doll?" I parted my fingers so she could breathe, but they're still clamped over her mouth. I peel them away now and turn her chin to see her eyes.

They are aware.

"Yes." She's back.

I pull out and clean us both up with some of the

napkins provided. Before I let her up, I spank her ass until it turns a pretty shade of pink.

"You got what you needed?" I ask.

When I let her up and see her face, it's transformed. There's color in her cheeks. Light behind her eyes. She smiles that wide smile at me.

"I'm much better, thank you."

I grip the sides of her face and kiss her. "I'm gonna take care of you, doll. Every time. You just have to let me."

She nods. "I want to."

*I want to.*

It's different than *I will*.

But it will have to do for now.

∽

*Caitlin*

I FEEL a million times better as we walk to the door of the sprawling estate. My ass is warm and tingly, my clit still pulses from the orgasm and all the feel-good chemicals are pumping through my veins.

I'm ready to marry Paolo on the spot for knowing what I needed.

Well, I would if I knew how to trust people, which I don't. I'm realizing that even if the Tacone family had nothing to do with my dad's death, I'm terrified of getting close to Paolo. Letting anyone in. I'm already so broken I don't believe I can rely on anyone but me. I don't want to make the mistake of believing I can only to have it not work out.

The woman who answers the door looks even younger than I am. "Hey, guys." She has a plump blonde baby girl on her hip and she pops the child higher before she leans forward and gives Paolo the double-cheek kisses.

"This is Caitlin, my girl. Be nice to her."

"When am I ever not nice?" The woman scoffs and pulls me into a one-armed hug. "It's great to meet you. I'm Alessia, the baby sister. Come on in."

I get nervous again inside. The giant living room is filled with the Tacone family and they all stop and look at us with interest.

"This is Vlad, my husband," Alessia says, when a tattooed man in shirtsleeves comes over and takes the baby from her. "And the baby is Lara. Our son Mika is over there." She points at a teenager who can't possibly be her real son. She couldn't have been more than ten when he was born.

Vlad shakes Paolo's and my hand and studies me with a piercing gaze. A shiver runs through me.

Paolo slides his arm around me and spreads his fingers across my belly, pulling me tightly against him. The message couldn't be more clear. I'm under his protection.

It feels nice.

Corey and Stefano come over to welcome us, then I'm introduced to Paolo's other brother, Nico, and his wife Sondra, a pretty blonde who also has a baby on her hip. "This is Nico Jr.," she tells me, kissing the baby's cheek.

"What can I get you to drink? A glass of wine? Cocktail?" Alessia offers.

For some reason, the thought of alcohol just turns my stomach. I swear I didn't have that much to drink last night, but I've been queasy all day. "Water would be great," I tell her.

"You want to put steaks on the grill?" Alessia suggests to Vlad.

Turns out it's code for all the men to go outside and stand around the grill while the women gather in the kitchen with wine.

Except when Mika gets sent back inside I know they're talking business out there.

Is it about my dad?

My queasiness kicks in even more. I pick up a cheese square from the hors d'oeuvres tray and pop it in my mouth.

"Did you have fun at the Bellissimo?" Corey asks.

I cringe. Small talk. *Awk*-ward. And I can't even pull out Crazy Caitlin to play. I want these women to like me.

What does that mean? Am I really seeing this thing with Paolo as a future?

That seems nuts, and yet... he means something to me.

"I had a great time. I've never been to Vegas at all, so Paolo made sure I got a taste of everything."

Alessia hands me a glass of water with lemon. "Not to freak you out, but Paolo's never showed up with a woman before. So we're all kind of fascinated to finally figure out his type."

"I don't think Caitlin's a type. I think she's an anomaly," Corey offers. To me she says, "You somehow cracked the Paolo code."

I tense, thinking she knows I'm a hacker, but I don't see any signs of it in her face.

"Nico was the same way, though," Alessia goes on. "No girlfriends and then suddenly—bam—he meets Sondra and knows she's *the one*."

"I-I don't know if I'm the one," I stutter in surprise. I try to picture myself here, part of their family, a baby on my hip. I can't see it.

"Yeah, no pressure. Sorry, I didn't mean to freak you out. I'm just happy to see Paolo happy."

I look at Paolo through the sliding glass door. It's Vegas, so they can stand out there without freezing even though it's December.

"How can you tell he's happy?" I ask doubtfully.

She laughs. "Well, connected, I guess. You're right, it's hard to tell what Paolo feels about anything. He keeps his cards pretty close to his chest. The way I tell is by his actions. If he brought you here, it's because you mean something to him."

I don't want to believe her. Because the idea of this thing actually working out terrifies me.

"I'll tell you something else about Paolo. He doesn't forge many connections. So when he does, they're powerful. He would do anything for the people he's decided he cares about. And I mean anything."

∽

*Paolo*

. . .

Vlad manages the steaks on the grill with his toddler on his hip. She leans into him, playing shy and watching us with big blue eyes. Every now and he speaks to her softly in Russian.

She's not Alessia's kid, but my sister couldn't be happier to be stepmom. Her health wouldn't have supported a pregnancy, so Lara and Mika—their adopted son—were a godsend.

I still want to beat the shit out of Vlad for kidnapping my sister and taking her to Russia, but I can't because he's family now. And I have to admit he's doing a damn good job making my baby sister happy.

"So you and the hacker. Didn't see that one coming," Nico says. "I thought I saw on the news she got picked up by the FBI. How'd she get out of jail?"

My hands curl into fists. "You got a problem with her?"

"I got no problem with her if you don't. This is your show, Paolo. The only thing I'm concerned about is the Feds connecting the two of you. Because you know they'd pick her up and put the screws to her in a heartbeat."

A wash of ice-cold rushes through me, even though I've already considered this possibility. Still, I don't like to hear it said out loud, especially not from Nico, who is probably the smartest and most tactical of all the Tacone brothers.

"I paid for Lucy Lawrence to go in anonymously. They won't trace it." Lucy's firm has handled our family's legal business since my father's era, but she took over our account about five years ago and impressed the shit out of all of us. She's a brilliant attorney who somehow maintains her humanity without being all high-moraled.

"Good," Nico says, but I get the feeling he doesn't believe it's all good.

"She wouldn't roll over, anyway," I say fiercely. But I'm not one hundred percent sure of that. She holds herself back. This could all be one giant manipulation.

"Whose idea was it to come to Vegas?" Nico's question is deceptively casual.

*Fanculo.*

"Hers. But she hasn't been out of my sight." Of course she was typing away on her computer this morning, and I have no way of knowing what the fuck she's doing on it.

The memory of her quizzing me over and over again about what I'd do if she betrayed me buzzes around in the back of my mind.

"There was no breach in security that I can see since you've been here," Vlad says with his thick Russian accent.

Well, that's good.

"She thinks the Family offed her dad," I tell them.

"No shit. Who's her dad?" Stefano asks.

"Lake West. Remember him? Small time middle man for stolen goods. Electronics mostly. That's what I've dug up, anyway. You know anything about his death?"

All three of them shake their heads.

"I think he could've been working for the *bratva*, too. Vlad, do you have ties to the other cells there? One that would've been around ten years ago when he disappeared?"

Vlad shrugs. "I can make an inquiry. Set up a meeting

if you like." After a moment's hesitation, he shakes his head. "They would kill you alone. I would have to come to Chicago and go with you to ensure your safety."

"Would you do that?"

Vlad shrugs. "You're family. My new brotherhood. Maybe Caitlin will be my new sister, ah?"

I look through the sliding glass doors at my crazy, wild unicorn of a girl. The geeky glasses perched on her nose somehow make the banging hot body even more banging. She's uncomfortable and I need to go in and rescue her soon.

"Something like that," I say, because it's hard to imagine Caitlin agreeing to marry me. But when he says it, I realize that's it. I'd love to lock this thing down with her forever. If I could be sure I trusted her. If I got to see all the secrets of her soul.

"Okay. I will set it up. We'll go next week." Vlad slides the cooked steaks onto a plate, which Stefano picks up, since Vlad's hands are full with Lara.

"Thank you, I appreciate that." I follow the men in and take up my protective position beside Caitlin.

My crazy, beautiful hacker unicorn.

The girl I'm not sure I can trust.

The girl I love.

CHAPTER 11

*Caitlin*

IN THE SILENCE between sex and sleep, Paolo's deep voice cracks the darkness.

"Who hurt you, doll?" We're spooning, my back to his front, his arm around me, hand molded over my breast.

I go still, listening to the sounds of our breath, making sure I know what he means. Even though I'm pretty sure I do, I warble, "What do you mean?"

He waits a beat. Then he says, "Tell me about the checking out thing."

My heart starts hammering. He must feel it because he shifts his hand to rest over my heart instead. His lips come to my nape. "Don't be afraid. Just tell me."

I don't know if *afraid* is the right word. But I'm broken. Damaged. And I don't like looking at my brokenness.

I lick my lips. "The official diagnosis is depersonalization-derealization disorder. It's one of the dissociative disorders. When I'm triggered, I have this out-of-body experience, not in a good way. Like I'm just an observer. Like you said, I check out."

"And who made you that way?"

Again, my heart-rate accelerates. Is it so obvious someone damaged me?

"Breathe," he commands, pinching my nipple, and I realize I was holding my breath. "Tell me."

He's so confident, so sure of himself. Six months of therapy and I could never bring myself to even hint that something happened. What if my therapist had just demanded the truth, like my dommy boyfriend? Would I have gotten over it?

I force my lips to move. "Wh-why?" I think I already know the answer.

"I'm going to avenge you."

My stomach somersaults. His solution is so simple. So obvious and overt. Someone wrongs you, there's retribution. I stole from him so I deserved to be kidnapped and have my brother threatened. It's like an equation or truth in his world.

How would I feel about my foster dad swimming with the fishes?

Actually, I'd be fine. I guess I have no moral compass, either. But I don't want him to commit murder for me.

"What will you do?"

"What do you want me to do?"

I suck in a long, shaky breath. I'm blanking out. Leaving my body.

When I don't answer, he says, "I'm trying to figure out if killing him will just traumatize you more."

"Maybe." I force the word across my lips. "Can you just beat him up?"

"Oh, I'll make him sorry he was born, doll. Give me his name."

My body starts to shake.

He holds me tighter. "I don't want make this worse, *bella.* I just want you to be free."

"Do it. Do it for me. I want you to." The shaking comes on harder. But I'm in my body, experiencing it.

It's a release of some kind. Like I'm shaking off every unwanted touch. Every cruelty I endured. It's some kind of rebirth as the fissured part of me I've been trying to keep together finally cracks apart.

"His name," he repeats in my ear.

"Andy Watson. My foster father." The room itself opens up and I drop into an abyss, free-falling through shame and awareness. Falling and falling and falling.

Until I land, squarely in Paolo's arms. Safe in bed. Protected. Defended.

Soon to be avenged.

"I love you, Paolo Tacone," I say into the darkness.

He kisses my neck and squeezes me even tighter. "You're my wildfire. I'm not gonna let anyone put out your light. Not ever."

〜

*Paolo*

. . .

Ravil Baranov, the boss of the *bratva*, lives near Gio in a high-rise apartment downtown on Lake Michigan. Actually, from what I gather, his entire cell inhabits the building, making it a Russian fortress.

Even the front door guy is covered in tattoos and greets us with a thick accent. Vlad speaks to him in Russian and we're both patted down.

I didn't wear a piece or even the brass knuckles I used to put Andy Watson in the hospital Monday. I made sure Caitlin's former foster dad will never touch another child. Not if he wants to live.

I haven't seen Caitlin since our flight home Sunday where she officially joined the Mile High club. She needed time to catch up on her work after being away all weekend, and I've been following up on the promises I made to her.

We take the elevator up to the top floor where we're patted down again by two surly tattooed men.

Ravil takes his security seriously. I respect that.

When we're finally led in, the head of the Russian *bratva* greets us in a sweater and a pair of jeans. His tattoos show on his knuckles and up his neck. The Russians use ink to mark every crime they commit. Every murder, every theft. Every act documented for their cell to see. Those with the most ink are the most dangerous.

He says something curt to Vlad and doesn't greet me at all. He just eyes me speculatively and says, "You asked for meeting. Why?"

"I'm looking for information about the death of a lowlife thief by the name of Lake West. Used to do a little business with both of us, I believe. I have no beef with his killer, I'm just making sure he's really dead."

Ravil's brows shoot up. I surprised him with the last part. "Killed by Tacone Family. That's what I heard." He shrugs. "You know something different?"

"I don't think we did it. But that's the word on the street. Thing is—there was no body discovered, so I'm wondering if it was faked. He owe you money?"

Ravil considers me for a minute before he nods slowly. "He was moving electronics for us. Your outfit was buyer. There was a double-cross and you killed him. We never got our money. We were new in town. We didn't want war with Tacones, so we didn't register complaint. West was dead, what could we do?"

I nod. The pieces are starting to come together. I have to say, I'd hoped Ravil would tell me they'd killed Lake West, but to me it all points to a faked death.

Except who would abandon his children for a lousy truck of stolen goods?

That man had better be dead or I'll make him wish he were when I find him.

~

*Caitlin*

I ROLL out of bed and run for the bathroom, but when I get there, I just dry heave.

Ugh. Three days I've been nauseous. This is getting so old.

I haven't had a drop to drink since Friday night at the Bellissimo, I really don't understand…

Oh fuck.

I yank open the drawer under the sink and stare at my packet of pills.

Sugar pills. Five gone. I should be bleeding now.

Dizzy, I throw the toilet seat down and sit on it.

Holy, holy crap.

I'm pregnant.

And it must be the hormones that make me feel like bursting into tears rather than dropping out of my body.

I gulp in my breath and release it slowly. Remember I have a pregnancy test under the sink from the last time I had a scare. It was a two-pack. I pull it out and pee on the stick.

Try to ignore the way the room spins when the pink plus sign appears.

Okay.

I'm pregnant. With Paolo's baby.

And he's not interested in having kids. There are suddenly too many disturbing possibilities crowding me. Would he ask me to get an abortion? Or would he support me keeping it?

I have a feeling if he did support me keeping it, we'd be locked in together. There'd be no getting out of our arrangement. He would own me for the rest of my life or at least until the kid was eighteen. Keeping this baby means keeping Paolo.

Forever.

A hitman for the mob.

I stuff my knuckles in my mouth as the tears hit hard. I don't know what to do. I can't tell Paolo. Not until I've had time to think through things.

Somehow, I get myself showered and ready for the day and out the front door.

And that's when my craptastic day gets even worse.

The two FBI agents who arrested me before are standing at my door.

"Ms. West? We need you to come in and answer some questions."

I don't feel a shred of remorse for puking on his shoes.

## CHAPTER 12

*Caitlin*

"I'm not saying a word without my lawyer present."

Yeah, I've watched a lot of crime television. Plus, I now have the experience of having had an actual, powerful lawyer in my court. And I want her here, right away.

"You aren't being charged with anything. We just have some questions for you, that's all," a female agent dressed in a silk button-down and starched slacks says from where she stands in the corner observing. Agent Docker, I think she said her name was. Her partner, a pompous weasel with bad teeth, sits across from me at the table. I missed his name.

I fold my arms across my chest. "Lawyer. Present."

Bad Teeth responds by sliding a blown-up photo in front of me. My mouth suddenly goes dry.

The photo is of my dad.

And Paolo.

And a few other guys I don't recognize—maybe his other brothers or soldiers.

They are standing in front of a coffee shop with awnings in the colors of the Italian flag and the sign Caffe Milano in script across the top.

I want to heave again.

"I need something to eat. Crackers or something. Unless you want me to puke on your photo."

Since Bad Teeth is the same guy who got puke on his shoes earlier, he sort of leaps back from the table and curses. "I'll find you something." He nods at Agent Docker and she nods back and takes the seat across from me.

"What we want to know is why you're screwing the guy who killed your father."

The words hit me like a cannonball, somewhere between my heart and my gut. My solar plexus, I guess.

I can't even breathe for a moment. All I can do is wheeze with the pain of it.

"H-how do you know he killed my father?"

"Everybody knew. It's common knowledge on the street, with the local police, and the FBI. The locals searched for the body so they could pin it on him, but he hid it too well. Probably buried in concrete like a lot of their vics.

I'm still wheezing. Barely able to get air in. "How do you know it was Paolo, specifically?"

The look she gives me is one part scorn, one part pity. "Seriously? They are all one family. You feel comfortable sleeping with the guy whose brother killed your dad? Or father? Or the guy who gave the order?" She shakes her head.

I stand up and heave.

"Oh shit," Agent Docker says and lurches for the garbage can, which she shoves in front of me.

I heave again, but nothing comes out.

I sink slowly back to my chair.

I'm suddenly cold. So freaking cold.

Ice cold.

"Listen, I get it. He's a good-looking and powerful man. I'm sure he's very suave. He's also good at making threats. He knows how to get people where it hurts so they do exactly what he wants them to. Is that what happened with you?"

It's hard to even think through the nausea. Plus, I'm starting to leave my body, which is a godsend at this point.

"Did Paolo pay you to hack into the Luxor?" she asks, but it's from far away. "Or did he blackmail you into it?"

I've retreated. Blessedly.

As if from underwater, I watch the other agent return with a granola bar, which he tosses on the table. I watch myself open it and eat it, tasting nothing.

It's dry and chews up the inside of my mouth, but I barely register that, either.

"We think you might be in trouble, Ms. West, and we want to help you."

"I'm sure you do," I hear myself say.

"He made you believe you were safe from the law. He sent in his expensive lawyer and made a deal that got you out, but let me tell you something, Ms. West. There's only one reason we let you walk, and that was to find out who you were working with. We figured it had to be someone big, but when we found out it was the guy who killed your father and left you and your brother in foster care, we figured you might be in trouble."

I barely hear them above the cotton stuffed in my ears. It doesn't matter what they say, anyway. I'm not listening. I don't have to.

The male agent leans forward. "We are fully prepared to bring all charges back against you for the Luxor crime. You're looking at twenty years in a Federal penitentiary. Are you prepared to rot in jail for the man who killed your own father?"

I don't answer.

"But if you're under duress, we can help. Has Paolo Tacone threatened you, your brother, or your livelihood in any way?"

The memory of him showing me the photo of my brother on his phone, warning me of what he's capable of, momentarily brings me back to my body with a flood of dread.

Even totally checked out, I know these two are all over the place. They don't know whether to play good cop or bad cop. They don't know what angle to chip away at.

I may be reeling, but I'm not stupid.

I'm not going to answer any of their questions.

Except maybe one. I lift my chin. "I'm only with Paolo Tacone because he fucks like a porn star. No other reason."

Bad Teeth's jaw drops. Then he frowns and gets up in my face. "You are in bed with the wrong man, Ms. West. And you're going to pay for it, dearly. I will bring charges against you that will send you to jail until you're too old to think about sex anymore. Or you can cooperate and help us put a dangerous killer behind bars. You decide."

The room spins. I look at the garbage can, trying to figure out if I'm going to need it again soon.

I stumble to my feet. From far away I hear myself say, "I'm leaving. You can't hold me here without charges or a call to my lawyer."

"We'll give you forty-eight hours to think this over," Bad Teeth says. "If we don't hear from you by then, we'll bring charges against you. Your choice."

My feet somehow move toward the door and they let me out, escorting me to the front door, both of them looking disgusted and having conversations with their eyes behind my back.

"Here's my card," Agent Docker says to me when we reach the front door. "Make the right decision."

I don't take the card. I don't even bother answering. I just push past them into the parking lot.

But once I'm there, I don't know where to go.

I don't even know how to function.

∞

*Paolo*

CAITLIN'S not in her apartment when I get there, which isn't unusual. It isn't quite 9:00 p.m. yet. Still, I have a strange prickling sense that something's off.

I didn't tell her I'd be here. I probably should have.

*All it takes is a little communication,* I hear my brother's words ringing in my ears.

I don't know why communication feels like a weakness. Like I'm admitting to something or giving up the upper hand.

Maybe she had plans with her friends tonight. Except that doesn't feel right. I stalked Caitlin enough to know she doesn't really have friends. She's friendly, she smiles and chit-chats with the people in her dance class or at school, but there's no one she's tight with except her younger brother.

I pull out my phone and dial her number.

It goes straight to voicemail.

Fuck.

I send a text instead, keeping it short. *Call me.*

I lie down on the bed to wait for her.

∽

*Caitlin*

*If it's business, I'm gonna deal with you in a business-like fashion. You talk to the Feds, we're done and the gloves come off.*

What if I get picked up by the feds but I don't talk to them?

Would he believe me? Or will he assume I'm wearing a wire?

What if I'm carrying the baby I don't want him to know about and the FBI wants me to rat on him or I'll go to jail for the next twenty years? What if I never get to see my own baby because I'm in jail and Paolo doesn't want it, either? Who's going to raise it?

I stand in the parking lot, immune to the bitter December wind blowing through the city. I'm out of my body, looking on like an observer.

*There's Caitlin. She's in quite a pickle. Good thing I don't have to deal with that shit.*

I don't know how long I stand there before I come to a hazy decision.

I can't go back to my apartment. I can't see Paolo until I figure my shit out. What to do about the pregnancy. What to do about the Feds.

Instead, I go to a coffee shop to hack into their credit card transactions. If the FBI are already building a case against me, what's one more transgression, right? I use the credit card to order a Lyft to take me on the two hour drive to Starved Rock.

Trevor will know where to find me if I decide not to come back. And once he does, we can both disappear. A hacker wields a power few truly understand—the ability to vanish and reinvent. I don't need the FBI to keep me safe. I can take care of myself. I always have.

Before I step outside to catch the Lyft, I buy myself a hot chocolate and a muffin. Because eating seems to help with the queasiness.

And I'm ready to puke my guts out.

## CHAPTER 13

*P*aolo

*Fanculo.* Where is she?

It's dark in the apartment. The clock says it's three in the morning. I don't even know how I slept without knowing where Caitlin was.

I surge out of bed and stalk through the apartment, checking my phone for messages, throwing on the lights.

Where in the fuck could she be?

I try calling her, but not surprisingly, there's no answer.

I'm ready to drive over to her brother's dorm and pull him out of bed, but I hold back. That would be harassment, and Caitlin wouldn't like it.

I start looking through the place more thoroughly, looking for signs. Her suitcase is still there—flung open but not unpacked from our trip to Vegas. Her computer equipment, but not her laptop. I go to her bathroom. I don't know what I'm looking for, but I look.

And that's when I see the box for a pregnancy test in the trash can. I pull it out. Below it is the actual test. I fish it out of the trash and look at the results.

*Madonna. Cristo. Dio.* She's pregnant!

Is that why she's not here? Where in the fuck did she go?

I go ice cold. Not because she's pregnant—I'd welcome that if it's what she wanted, but because she didn't turn to me with this knowledge. She ran away.

It chills me to the bone and makes me crazy to find her, to give her whatever she needs to get through this decision. To let her know she's fully supported no matter what.

I start for the door a dozen times, then sit back down. I want to be here if she comes to the apartment.

I wait until dawn breaks. Until the traffic outside becomes a roar. Until there's no denying she's not coming back. Pocketing the pregnancy test, as if keeping that evidence with me will somehow help me find her, I leave and head to her old apartment, to see if she's holed up there.

She isn't.

My phone rings at 8:30 a.m. and I see it's Nico. We don't chitchat, he and I, so I know it's business, and because of this thing with Caitlin, I nearly crack the phone I grip it so hard.

"Nico."

"I got a call from my informant at the FBI."

I didn't think it was possible for me to go colder, but I do.

"What is it?"

"They picked up your girl yesterday and brought her in. She stayed about three hours and then they let her go. That's all I know."

I want to roar with the pain piercing my chest. Did she betray me? All those questions about what I'd do in different scenarios. Was it because she was already working with the feds? Or because she knew she would?

I force breath through my nostrils.

"She's fucking MIA, Nico," I tell him, my entire being cracking in half. "She's MIA and she's pregnant with my child."

Nico curses in Italian.

I slam my forehead against the plaster wall and crack it.

I loved that girl.

I still do.

*And she's pregnant.*

"Well, if she's missing that means she didn't roll over," Nico says, thinking faster than I am. "If she rolled, she'd be by your side wearing a fucking wire. She wouldn't disappear and raise flags. She probably got scared between the pregnancy and pressure from the feds and she ran."

*Away* from me? Why?

She's still scared of me.

This is all my fucking fault. I couldn't show her enough of myself for her to feel safe. To know I'd never hurt her in a million years.

I keep sucking in my breath, processing Nico's words. They make sense. "Yeah, you're right."

"So you gotta figure out where she would go. What can I do to help?"

Right. I gotta figure this shit out. My shoulders crack as I square them. I will fucking find her. I will find her and let her know she doesn't have to run.

"Find out what happened while she was with the feds, if you can."

"Yeah, already on it, but my informant didn't have clearance. He's going to try, though."

"Well, let me know if you find anything. I'm going to go shake down—I mean, have a conversation—with her brother. If anyone knows where she would be, it would be him."

"Yeah. Go find her. Everything's gonna be all right."

I know if Nico is offering me comfort, my cracks are showing. And I don't give a shit.

"Yeah. Thanks. I'll keep you posted."

"Likewise."

## CHAPTER 14

*Caitlin*

I MADE a huge mistake coming here. Like colossal.

For one thing, it looks like someone found the hidden key and made themselves at home sometime in the last two years. That's how long it's been since I've been here.

It's suddenly very clear to me I was stupid to keep this place. It was the only thing Trevor and I inherited from our dad when he died. After they declared him dead, the judge ordered for the land to be sold to pay for our care, but it didn't sell right away.

And that was when I got serious about hacking. It was a skill I'd already been honing. So I just electronically removed the cabin sale from the government auction and kept it. I put the water, gas and electric on the government's tab. I don't feel bad since we don't use much.

Still, I've hung onto it as the one thing we have to our

names. This place of our own we could come to if we ever needed to hide out or get away.

Right now, though, I'm wishing we'd sold it and taken the money.

The place is a dump. It's falling apart. Maybe I'm just creeped out by the fact that someone else has been here. I can tell by the cigarette butts and empty beer bottles. The pair of men's jeans draped across the unmade bed.

I couldn't sleep at all last night worrying that whoever it was might be coming back, even though there are no signs that they were here recently.

But the real problem is that I was in such a state of trauma last night, I didn't even bring any food. My hunger quickly morphed into queasiness and I've been throwing up water all morning.

Add to that the very enormous problem that my phone signal's not working, which means no hotspot or WiFi. No internet.

So now I'm literally stranded here.

In a cabin, in the snow, miles from civilization.

With no food.

If I thought being knocked up by a mobster and hauled in by the feds was bad, I had no idea.

I may not make it out of here alive.

*Paolo*

FROM CAITLIN'S OLD APARTMENT, it's a short trip to Trevor

West's dormitory. I wait outside until he comes out, and then I join him on the sidewalk, matching his pace.

He takes one sidelong look at me and lurches away.

"Don't run," I command, because I don't want to grab him. Assaulting Caitlin's brother probably isn't going to help things.

He freezes, but only because he thinks I'm holding a piece on him. I know, because his eyes instantly dart to my hands. When he sees they're free, he starts to turn again.

"I said, *hold up*," I growl.

He hesitates.

"You know who I am?" I don't have any idea how much Caitlin's told him. If he even knows about us.

"I have a guess," he says, wary as hell.

"I'm the guy who's in love with your sister," I say.

That stops him. No, he definitely didn't expect those words. His eyes snap to mine. They are the same shade of cornflower blue as hers. His dark hair hangs over them like shutters. He's a good-looking kid in an emo kind of way.

"Listen, I need your help."

Wariness returns to his face and he shifts his stance like he's ready to run for it again.

"Have you heard from Caitlin? Since yesterday? She's missing and I—"

"I don't know where she is," he says immediately, ducking his head and hunching his shoulders up against the wind. He starts walking away from me.

He's lying. I always know when they're lying and this kid's easy to read.

Once again, I resist the urge to grab his arm and yank him back, instead matching his pace, then step in front of him to block his path. "*Listen* to me. She got picked up by the feds yesterday."

That gets his attention. He definitely didn't know. But he still doesn't trust me, because now he seems even more determined to get away. Fear flickers over his face. I know how this must seem. If all this kid knows about me is that I'm the guy who killed his dad, he's not gonna see me as an ally.

"I'm not going to hurt her." I thrust my hand in my jacket pocket and produce the pregnancy test. I hold it in front of his face. "She's carrying my child."

He goes still, looking from the pregnancy test to me. "I never heard a word about you," he says suspiciously.

"Well, maybe she wasn't proud of it." It hurts me to say it out loud. To acknowledge that the woman I love has such a big hang-up with giving herself to me. "She knows I'm not responsible for your dad's death."

I need to get that out of the way. If he sees me as his dad's killer, he's never going to talk.

"Listen. I think she's probably freaked out right now. She just found out she's pregnant, and I'm guessing the feds put pressure on her to turn informant. They probably threatened her with renewing the charges. If she was scared and needed to figure shit out, where would she go?"

His mouth is tight as he looks over my shoulder stonily, like he's thinking. "There's a place," he says finally.

"Where?"

"I'm going with you."

Okay, sure. He doesn't trust me. "Fine," I say curtly. "Get in my SUV."

*Caitlin*

I CRANK up the heat and put some hot water on to boil. There's a ten-year-old can of instant coffee here that I know is going to make me even more miserable to drink, but I have to try it.

My head aches. My breasts are tender. I feel seasick.

And for once, I don't appreciate being fully seated in my body experiencing it all. But I can't tap out or I may not survive. I need to get my wits together and make a plan.

So far all I've come up with is walking until I get a phone or WiFi signal. But considering there's a freaking blizzard outside, that plan could mean a quicker death than staying inside and starving.

It's funny how being in a life or death situation sharpens everything to a fine point. I have clarity now.

I want the baby.

The instinct to protect the tiny life inside me changed everything. I've been far too reckless with my life, right up to my arrival here. But no more. There's more at stake than one crazy woman. There's a tiny, defenseless, innocent being relying on me for survival.

And I'd give anything right now to be able to call Paolo. For one thing, I know he'd rescue me in a heartbeat. For another... well, I don't know what he'll say about the pregnancy, but he deserves to know. We should have a conversation.

I shouldn't have been scared of him or what he'd do. Even if he heard about the FBI picking me up, he'd give me a chance to explain what happened. He's going to believe I wouldn't turn informant.

The feds sucker-punched me with the photo of him with my dad, but it doesn't prove anything. They were looking for any way to manipulate me.

The water boils and I pour some into a mug, then add the instant coffee and stir. My stomach turns. Ugh. Maybe I won't be able to choke this down.

Outside, I hear the sound of a car. Grabbing my coat, I dash outside. Whoever it is, I need to flag them down.

An old pickup pulls down the dirt drive with two passengers. I squint to make out the face of the driver.

No.

It can't be.

I stumble back and fall flat on my ass onto the porch steps.

Well, at least I know one thing with total certainty: Paolo definitely didn't kill my dad.

No, he's living and breathing and parking a pickup truck right in front of the damn cabin.

~

*Paolo*

IT TAKES three and a half hours driving through a blizzard to arrive at what Trevor simply calls, "the cabin". I drove my Rover, so we can at least manage the snow, but even with four-wheel drive, I slip and slide in places.

Every minute that passes, the gnawing dread in my gut grows larger. What if she's not here? Then we just wasted the entire day driving out here to find her. Also—what if she is? I hate that she ran so far away. Is she really that afraid of me? How did she get here? I know she doesn't know how to drive.

And I can't even face my ultimate fear—that I won't have the words to make her see I'm on her side. That she'll choose to stay gone.

I want to say I won't accept that. But it's that character trait of mine that made her run. I can't bulldoze myself into someone's life. Well, I've obviously done exactly that, but I have to stop. I can't make her want me. And bottom line, if I truly care about her, I have to respect her wishes if she really wants to be free of me.

*Fanculo.*

There are fresh tire tracks in the snow on the unpaved road Trevor directs me to. I hope to fuck they belong to the car that brought her here, although a million questions rage over who drove it and why they're fresh. She's been missing since last night, so if she got here yesterday, they'd be snowed over by now.

Fuck, I'm definitely overthinking.

"It's right here," Trevor says, pointing to a dilapidated old cabin—barely worthy of the name. A rusty pickup sits in front of the house.

"Who owns the truck?" I demand. If I were a dog, my hackles would be raised and I'd already be growling protectively.

"I don't know." Trevor ducks his head to peer through the large window in the front.

I park and turn off the vehicle.

But then I think he recognizes the person because Trevor lunges quickly and grabs for the gun I keep under my seat. Smart kid. He must've noticed it earlier. My reflexes kick in before I even process what's happening. I smash his wrist against the dash. The gun drops into my lap.

"*Porca puttana!*" I tuck the weapon in my waistband in the back. "You're lucky I didn't break your fucking wrist." We both get out of the SUV. "You're also lucky I'm in love your sister or I would fuck you up for that. Who's in there?"

He looks at me sharply, like he's surprised I figured out that he knows.

He swallows.

*"Tell me."*

"It looks like... someone who's supposed to be dead."

*Minchia.*

Just what we need right now—a fucking family reunion. I have to say, though, I'm not surprised. I had a feeling the little fucker was still alive.

I palm the gun and try the front door. It's open, which surprises me. Lake West and a skanky woman are on their feet, jackets still on like they just arrived. Caitlin stands opposite them. When I see Caitlin's pale face and dead eyes, I forget everything but getting my arms around her.

Lake recognized me and his eyes fly wide with terror. Because yeah. He thinks I want him dead. He draws a weapon at the same time I do.

Fuck.

I should lower my weapon. This is Caitlin's father. I don't trust him not to shoot me though. Not until I explain I'm not after him, I'm here for Caitlin.

"Hold up, both of you," Trevor commands.

"Who the fuck are you?" Lake snaps.

"Of course you wouldn't recognize your own son," Trevor mutters.

I need to take fucking charge of this situation. "Listen, West. I didn't come here to kill you," I say evenly. "I came for Caitlin. And the baby of mine she's carrying." I drop that bomb to convey to West the nature of our relationship, in case he doesn't know.

Surprise definitely registers on Lake's face. I can't focus on Caitlin, but I sense her surprise too.

"You know?" she asks.

"Yeah, I know. Is that why you left, doll?" I shift my focus to her face for a fraction of a second.

A mistake.

Lake lunges for her and puts her in a headlock, holding the gun to her head.

I want to howl in rage. How stupid was I to let him know what matters to me? To assume he would care about his daughter and unborn grandchild as much as I do? Or be smart enough to reason that I'm not a threat.

I hold my gun steady. I could shoot him. I have a clear shot and I'm confident in my aim. But I can't risk Caitlin's life. Plus, he's still her dad, even if he's the lowest of the low.

I release my finger from the trigger and turn the gun to the side, moving slowly. "Okay, West. I'm putting the gun down." I set it on the coffee table. "Now put yours down. You're scaring your daughter." I purposely use those words, trying to appeal to his fatherly instincts, although he clearly has none.

He doesn't lower the gun, but he does shift to point it at me. I see it all in slow motion.

His finger squeezes the trigger. Caitlin grabs his wrist. I lunge to the side.

The bullet goes through the window.

In a second, I'm on him, knocking the gun out of his hand and slamming my fist into his face. He goes down and I follow, pounding with both my fists. This man held a gun to my girl's head. He left her to that monster of a foster father at age fourteen.

He's gonna pay.

~

*Caitlin*

I'M SO FAR OUT of my body, I'm on Mars. I see the scene unfolding from far, far away. Trevor still standing there with a gun in his shaking hand.

My dad on his back getting the shit beat out of him by Paolo.

His bitch of a girlfriend shrinking in the corner with terror in her eyes.

And I feel nothing.

A better person would stop Paolo. Or at least a living one. But I'm not better and I'm definitely not present.

And if I did feel anything, I'm pretty sure it would be satisfaction that my dad is getting his due.

All this time, he's been alive.

*What are you doing here, Caitie?* was all he had to say to me when he got out of his pickup. Like I don't belong here. Like he resented me being here. No explanation or apology for ditching out on his two kids when they were the ripe old age of eight and fourteen. For leaving us to become wards of the state. To rot in foster care while he was off living large.

*What are* you *doing here?* I shot back and he had the audacity to say, *this place belongs to me.*

The thud of bone cracking bone trickles into my awareness. Blood splatters on the floor. It's amazing how many punches a guy can take and still be conscious. Still be breathing.

I wonder if Paolo will kill him.

And it's only the memory of not wanting Paolo to kill for me when he offered to take care of my foster father that makes me reach out and touch his arm.

I expect him to shake me off. Or to not even notice me because he's in warrior zone, but the moment I touch him, he straightens, turns and pulls me into his arms.

I want to feel it. I can tell it would be nice to be held by Paolo right now. That I've been in need of his strength and protection. He rubs my back. I wish I could feel it.

But I'm way too out of my body to feel the warmth of his touch.

"What do you want me to do with him," I hear him ask from far away.

I make my lips move. "Let's go."

"No, he goes." Paolo turns and kicks my dad in the ribs. "This cabin is yours. He's dead. He has no rights to it." He kicks him again, then reaches down and hauls him up with his fists in his clothing.

"You'd better stay dead this time, West. Because the *bratva* will be looking for you for that truck full of electronics you stole. And if I ever see you again?" He says something menacing in Italian. "I'll fucking skin you alive, you greedy little weasel. You abandoned your kids for a couple hundred grand?" He cocks his fist back and delivers another vicious blow, then shoves him in the direction of his girlfriend.

"Get him out of here," he tells the girlfriend. "And don't fucking come back."

Out-of-body Caitlin watches them stumble out. I'm so fucking numb. So removed. Vaguely, it occurs to me that I need to get back. And Paolo's here.

He knows how to do it.

He turns to me, his face etched with concern. I pick up his meaty hand and put it on my throat, pressing in to squeeze.

*Choke me.* My silent plea.

He understands. He cups the back of my head and leans his lips down to my temple. "I would, doll, but I think your brother will shoot me."

Observer Caitlin notes Trevor still gripping Paolo's pistol. "Put the gun down," I hear myself say.

I don't feel the relief I know I should when he starts and sets it down on the coffee table like it's a snake.

There's something else. Something I need. Oh yeah.

"I'm hungry," I force the words across my lips.

Paolo sweeps the kitchen with his gaze, then shakes his head. "Let's get you out of here." He scoops me into his arms. "We passed a lodge not too far from here. We can get a meal and stay there until the storm passes."

I see Trevor's pale face as Paolo turns with me. How did he get here? Oh yeah, he showed up with Paolo.

How did Paolo get here?

"Do I need to shut the water off, Caitie?" Trevor asks.

The water… I can't figure out what that means.

"I'll get it. Be out in a minute," he tells Paolo.

Paolo carries me to a shiny Range Rover and carefully sits me in the passenger seat. He pulls the seatbelt across my waist and buckles it.

I need to tell him things. Lots of things.

I make my tongue work. "They showed me pictures. The FBI. Pictures of you and him. They told me you killed him."

Pain flickers on Paolo's face.

"I didn't believe them." There. That's what I wanted to tell him.

He catches my gaze and holds it. "I will never lie to you, Cait."

And the strangest thing happens.

I drop back into my body for a moment. Warmth spreads across my chest. I find my way back to the present through love, not pain.

As I start to recede again, I reach for more. "I love you," I blurt.

It's not my declaration, but what I see on Paolo's face that brings me back this time. Tears pop into his eyes—I swear to God. He blinks rapidly and lunges in for me.

Captures my head in both his hands and holds me captive for a searing kiss.

A claiming kiss. His lips move brutally across mine, his tongue lashes my mouth. He pours all his powerful presence, his life force, his protection into me.

The warmth spreads more. Into my belly. Down my arms. Pooling in my pelvis.

When he pulls away, I'm back. I'm sitting on the car seat, freezing my ass off while my huge, handsome lover stands over me.

"They want me to turn informant." I have to get the worst of it out. Make sure he knows and understands I would never betray him. "They say I have forty-eight hours to decide or they'll bring charges against me."

He shakes his head. "They're bluffing, doll. But if they do, we'll handle it. We have Lucy in our court and she's the very best defense attorney there is. I'm not going to let you go to jail again. Not ever. *Lo prometo.*"

I don't understand Italian, but he'd translated the phrase for me before. It was his promise, his solemn vow.

He strokes his thumb down my cheek. "Is that why you ran?" His expression is so tender—no anger or hardness at all.

I'm surprised by a tear falling. No pain. No punishment. I'm feeling feelings just like that.

"Or was it because of this?" He holds up the pregnancy test.

"Yeah. Both," I croak.

"Talk to me, *bella.* Why did you run? You scared of me?"

"I just—" I shiver and he reaches across me to put the key in the ignition and start the vehicle.

"Yes, I got scared. Confused. I didn't know what I wanted. And I didn't think you'd want the baby—you told me you never wanted kids. And I didn't know what I would do if you didn't. I don't know you well enough, Paolo. Would you force me into something? To abort it? Or if I kept it, would you call all the shots?"

I usually can't read him at all, but I'm sure it's grief that makes Paolo close his eyes and his shoulders sag.

"Fuck!" He balls his fists and shouts up to the sky. He thumps his forehead on the frame of the Range Rover.

Trevor appears behind him, but Paolo stays him with an outstretched finger. He doesn't look from my face, though.

"I will never force you. And I know I have. I got you put in jail and I'm sorry for that—it was a mistake. I'll make it up to you.

"Caitlin, I'm sorry you don't know me well enough to feel safe. I'm shit at showing my feelings or even sharing my thoughts. But this is all you need to know: I'm your man. I may talk tough. I know I *am* tough. I like to be in charge and tell you how things are going to go. But bottom line, I'm your man. That means I have your back. I'm gonna protect you and make sure you're happy, no matter what. So ultimately, doll? *You* call the shots. I'm gonna show up for you however you want. If you want to keep this baby, I will be the best fucking dad you could dream of. If you decide you can't deal, I'll be by your side through that, too. It's your body, your life. You get to decide."

Fresh tears drip down my cheeks. I'm utterly demolished by his words. No one's ever showed up for me like this before. I've never had anyone I could count on except myself.

"I love you," I whisper. The words are new to say. Each time lights a flame behind Paolo's eyes.

I get a repeat of the kiss he gave me before, but shorter this time because I shiver.

"Let's get out of here before we get snowed in." He waves to Trevor and they both pile in the car.

When we reach the state highway, we pass my dad's truck, stuck in the snow. Paolo drives by without comment. Neither Trevor nor I say a word.

He left us to fend for ourselves when we had no way to protect ourselves. He can find his own way out of his messes.

∽

*Paolo*

A HOT MEAL and the warm lodge does everybody good. Caitlin's color returns and she gets a little life back in her. No one says much of anything until our plates are empty. Then Trevor puts down his fork and looks at Caitlin. "What the fuck."

"I know, right?"

"Did you know he was alive?"

"Of course not," Caitlin sputters.

"Was he at the cabin when you got there?" Trevor asks.

Caitlin shakes her head. "He showed up today, just a few minutes before you guys did. He had the nerve to ask *me* what I was doing there."

"You've gotta be kidding me. And then he held a gun to your head."

They both stare at each other for a moment as if shocked anew by what went down. "And my first thought was to protect Dad. I thought maybe this was all just his elaborate scheme to draw Dad out and kill him." He tips his head in my direction. "Sorry, man."

"No hard feelings. How's the wrist?"

He pulls back his sleeve and reveals a bruise blooming on his pale skin.

Caitlin gasps. "What did you do?"

"I went for his gun." Trevor rubs his wrist. "It's fine. Thanks for not killing me."

I sit back in my chair. "You have immunity."

Caitlin's eyes go soft and warm on me and it does something crazy to my chest. It tightens and expands it at the same time.

This woman... the things she does to me. Over the course of the last twenty-four hours I've been to hell and back thinking I might be losing her. I still don't know if I've won her over yet.

"Did you know, Paolo? What was the thing you said about the Russians?" Caitlin asks.

"Yeah, I suspected. I've been asking around. Before your dad supposedly was killed by my family, he screwed over the Russians. Stole a semi-truck full of electronics he was supposed to fence for them. They stopped looking for him when they heard we killed him. And since I knew we didn't do it, I figured it was a well-laid plan to disappear with a couple hundred grand. I just don't understand how a man could leave his two kids behind with no one to take care of them."

"And I stole from you thinking I was balancing the scales." Caitlin winces. "Sorry, big man."

I shake my head. "I'm not sorry," I tell her. "Shaking you down is the highlight in my long and illustrious career as the family enforcer."

Trevor cringes. "I'm sure I don't want to know how that went down."

"Nope, you don't." I toss some cash on the table and stand. "Now I'm gonna steal your sister for a while." I take Caitlin's hand and help her to stand. She weaves her fingers through mine. "We'll meet you back here for a late dinner."

"Yep. See you later. Have fun."

*Caitlin*

"I NEED A SHOWER," I declare the minute we're in the suite. If Paolo's going to exercise his rights to my body, I need to get clean.

The suite's gorgeous—rustic in design but with all the amenities, including a gas fireplace, which Paolo promptly fires up.

I head into the bathroom and strip off my clothes.

Paolo's right behind me. When he climbs into the

shower I feel suddenly shy. Exposed. Vulnerable. Like this is the first time we've been naked together instead of the twenty-seventh.

Maybe it's because so much has changed between us. I'm not looking at Paolo as a play partner or a sex partner. I'm not viewing this as a sugar daddy situation or something more coercive than that.

We're talking about love now.

About two people who made a baby together. Who are angling for spending their lives together.

My breath quickens as he steps into me, crowding me back against the cool tile. He picks up the soap and rolls it in his palm, his eyes never leaving my face.

"Are we good?"

His gaze is magnetic. I nod, drawn into the intensity of his regard. He strokes across my collarbone, spreading the soap he gathered in his palm. He traces down my arm. Underneath it. Across my breast, stopping to strum my nipple with his thumb. Every touch is reverential. Honoring. Like I'm a goddess and he's worshipping at my altar.

The trembling starts in my knees, but it spreads through my core, my belly, down my arms. I keep expecting him to turn savage, to throw me up against the tile and fuck me hard, but he never does. He soaps my entire body, every inch, every crevice, until I'm clean. Then he turns off the spray and steps out.

He wraps a towel around me and uses the two ends to pull me up against his burly body for a kiss. I kiss him back like it's our first kiss. Like it's our first date and I'm just learning to taste him.

We built our romance backward—starting with his belt

across my ass and zip tie bondage. Ending—no, not ending, but arriving here. Me trembling before him. Finally ready to give myself.

Not my body, but my whole self. My heart. My trust. My life to him.

He dries me off, stopping to kiss me again and again. Then walks me backward until I hit the bed. Even there, he remains gentle, lifting me to place me on my back before climbing over me.

He dips his head to suckle one nipple as he toys with the other. They're both sensitive from the hormones, and I feel the answering tug in my core almost immediately.

I arch on the bed. "Paolo."

He rubs the head of his cock between my legs, and I spread them and lift my hips to take him in. He plunges deep.

"Look at me." His command penetrates straight into my bones.

I lift my eyes to meet his. I hadn't realized I wasn't looking, but now that our gazes lock, I squirm at the vulnerability. Of being so very bared to him as he rocks slowly into me.

"I know you don't like it basic, but this is what you're getting."

There's my tough guy.

Swoon.

"Who's gonna make you come like a porn princess?"

I smile. "You are."

"That's right." He plunges even deeper, but his strokes remain smooth. No slamming home or pounding. "Who's going to take care of you for the rest of your life?"

I nearly crack open at that. I can't bear how raw those words make me feel, so I sit up to wrap my arms around his neck. To bury my face there.

He puts his hand around my throat and pushes me back down to the bed. "Look at me." Now his true nature starts showing itself. He rocks in harder, more insistently. "Who, doll?"

"You are?" I whisper, lips trembling.

"That's right. Even from the fucking grave. I'm your man, *bella.* I'm gonna take care of you."

His words imprint onto my soul, and I'm utterly humbled by them. I feel undeserving of such devotion. "Why me?"

He just smiles. "You're my wildfire. You're you. That's all it is. You're the woman for me. I knew you were special from the first time I saw your photo. Before I even showed up at your place. But I was unprepared for how much of an effect you'd have on me. How much you'd change me. I'm yours, doll. This is it for me. And I'm gonna keep working until you believe in me. Until you trust what we have."

Tears spill from my eyes. "I believe. I totally believe. I just don't know how I got so lucky," I choke.

Paolo strokes his thumb across my lower lip. "I'm the lucky one." He pulls one of my knees up to my chest to change the angle of entry and picks up his pace.

I drag my lip between my teeth, savoring the sensations, reveling in the confident way he handles me and my body. Even if he's not rough, he's always dominant.

"Look at me."

I find his eyes again. "No more running."

"I won't. I promise."

He pushes me to my belly and enters from behind. Now he finally gives it to me the way I like it, pinning my arms behind my back and holding my elbows as he rides me. "Come, little hacker," he commands when he gets close.

"You first," I say.

He fucks me hard, slapping his loins against my ass until I can't help but come, and as soon as I do, he finishes, shoving deep and staying there while I tighten around him.

He eases his hold on my arms and lowers himself over my body. His lips find my neck. His teeth nip me.

Aftershocks ripple through me, and I squeeze his cock until I force it out.

"I love you." I like saying it. I like what those words to do my chest. How they reverberate in my body. The effect they have on him.

He bites me hard. He doesn't like to say it back. He hasn't. But I don't care. He shows me. Like his sister said—his actions speak for him.

He drops to his side. "Look at me."

I turn my head to face him.

He looks me right in the eyes. "I love you."

There's a promise there. An oath. A swearing. I feel the words right down to my toes. In my core. In my cells.

He strokes his hand over my ass and the backs of my legs, a gentle exploring. "I'm gonna punish you for running," he rumbles.

My grin is ear-wide. "Promise?"

He squeezes my ass roughly.

"Thank God. I was afraid you were going to treat me like a delicate flower now that I'm pregnant."

He strokes my temple. "I might. I might do whatever the fuck I like with you."

My smile widens. "There he is."

He gives me one of those rare smiles.

"Paolo?"

His brow quirks.

"Do you want to be a dad?" I ask.

He opens his mouth, then shuts it. Then opens it again. "I want whatever you do. I mean it."

"No, really. I want to know." I realize he's not going to tell me one way or the other. If he's decided being my man means supporting me with whatever I choose, he won't want to sway me. "Just tell me the truth. What was your first thought when you saw the pee stick?"

"Well, I was scared as shit because you were missing, doll. And I was just focused on what the news meant to you. But now that you're here… I'm really fucking excited about the idea. I never thought I wanted kids, but that's because I was never in love before. I mean the idea of multiplying you? Have more little Caitlins running around?" He hits his fist to his chest like he can't even speak he's so overcome.

My vision blurs. "Yeah?" I give a watery laugh. "What if they're little Paolos?"

"Well, the poor bastards would be as lucky as I am to get to live with you."

"Are we living together now?"

"Fuck, yes, we're living together. Are we having this baby?"

"Yes." Tears drip down my face. "Yes, I want to. But I don't want to quit school or dance cardio or anything. I don't know, I guess I want it all."

"Then you'll have it all." Paolo pushes me to my side and snugs me up against him, face to face. "I'll handle it."

The tears fall harder. Explosions of celebrations go off in my chest. "Yeah? We're going to do this? We're having this baby?"

Paolo kisses me. "*I'm* having *you*," he says firmly. "And yeah, we're having a baby." After a moment, he says, "Don't freak out when I move you again."

"Isn't it too soon? What if I lose the baby? Twenty percent of pregnancies end in miscarriage."

Paolo goes still, like he's never contemplated that possibility. Then he answers with total Paolo confidence, "If that happens, I'll knock you up again, doll. I'm having this family."

He tips my chin up. "You worried I'm too old? I meant it when I said I'll take care of you from the grave. No one will ever touch you. You'll be provided for. You become a Tacone, you'll have my family behind you for life."

"Are you proposing?"

He goes still again. "You're mine. But, yes, I am going to put a ring on that finger. Are you ready to say yes?"

I laugh and roll to my back. It seems huge, but also, it's nothing. I've already accepted I'm his. And I knew that meant every part of me, because this man doesn't half-ass anything.

"Maybe," I murmur.

"'Kay." Paolo's not offended. He always accepts me

where I am. It's a gift I never expected. One few people ever receive.

"I love you," I say again, turning back to him. Still adoring those three words.

He smiles. "*Ti amo, bella.*"

I gasp. "Can we honeymoon in Italy?"

His laugh fills the room. "Of course. Anything you want, doll."

I sit up, suddenly excited about all the possibilities. About my future with Paolo. "What are we doing for Christmas?"

"Vegas, baby. The whole family takes over the top floors of the Bellissimo."

"Can Trevor come?"

"He's family now."

I beam at him.

He spreads his hands. "What else? Your wish is my command."

My smile gets even bigger. "I'm ready for my punishment now."

Paolo's eyes go dark and he pounces, pinning me back down and rolling me to my belly. "Punishment, it is, little girl."

~

THANK you for reading the final book in the Vegas Underground series. I'm sad to say goodbye to the Tacones (unless I come back for a next generation round?). Make sure you're signed up for my newsletter to get the Tacone

Family Christmas bonus scene (I'll send it out on Christmas day).

I'll be continuing with Ravil, the head of the Chicago *bratva* and Lucy, Paolo's attorney in the first book in the new spin-off Chicago Bratva series. Stay tuned for its release!

## WANT FREE RENEE ROSE BOOKS?

Click here to sign up for Renee Rose's newsletter and receive a free copy of *Theirs to Protect, Owned by the Marine*, *Theirs to Punish, The Alpha's Punishment, Disobedience at the Dressmaker's* and *Her Billionaire Boss*. In addition to the free stories, you will also get special pricing, exclusive previews and news of new releases.

## ABOUT RENEE ROSE

**USA TODAY BESTSELLING AUTHOR RENEE ROSE** loves a dominant, dirty-talking alpha hero! She's sold over a half million copies of steamy romance with varying levels of kink. Her books have been featured in USA Today's *Happily Ever After* and *Popsugar*. Named Eroticon USA's Next Top Erotic Author in 2013, she has also won *Spunky and Sassy's* Favorite Sci-Fi and Anthology author, *The Romance Reviews* Best Historical Romance, and *Spanking Romance Reviews'* Best Sci-fi, Paranormal, Historical, Erotic, Ageplay and favorite couple and author. She's hit the *USA Today* list five times with various anthologies.

**Please follow her on:**
**Bookbub | Goodreads**

*Renee loves to connect with readers!*
www.reneeroseromance.com
reneeroseauthor@gmail.com

OTHER TITLES BY RENEE ROSE

**Vegas Underground Mafia Romance**

*King of Diamonds*

*Mafia Daddy*

*Jack of Spades*

*Ace of Hearts*

*Joker's Wild*

*His Queen of Clubs*

*Dead Man's Hand*

*Wild Card*

**More Mafia Romance**

*The Russian*

*The Don's Daughter*

*Mob Mistress*

*The Bossman*

**Contemporary**

*Fire Daddy*

*Hollywood Daddy*

*Her Royal Master*

*The Russian*

*Black Light: Valentine Roulette*

*Black Light: Roulette Redux*

*Black Light: Celebrity Roulette*

*Theirs to Protect*

*Scoring with Santa*

*Owned by the Marine*

*Theirs to Punish*

*Punishing Portia*

*The Professor's Girl*

*Safe in his Arms*

*Saved*

**Paranormal**

**Bad Boy Alphas Series**

*Alpha's Temptation*

*Alpha's Danger*

*Alpha's Prize*

*Alpha's Challenge*

*Alpha's Obsession*

*Alpha's War*

*Alpha's Mission*

*Alpha's Sun*

***Shifter Fight Club***

*Alpha's Desire*

*Alpha's Bane*

*Alpha's Secret*

*Alpha's Prey*

### ***Midnight Doms***

*Alpha's Blood*

### ***Alpha Doms Series***

*The Alpha's Hunger*

*The Alpha's Promise*

*The Alpha's Punishment*

### **Other Paranormals**

*His Captive Mortal*

*Deathless Love*

*Deathless Discipline*

*The Winter Storm: An Ever After Chronicle*

### **Sci-Fi**

### **Zandian Masters Series**

*His Human Slave*

*His Human Prisoner*

*Training His Human*

*His Human Rebel*

*His Human Vessel*

*His Mate and Master*

*Zandian Pet*

Their Zandian Mate

*His Human Possession*

**Zandian Brides (Reverse Harem)**

*Night of the Zandians*

*Bought by the Zandians*

*Mastered by the Zandians*

*Zandian Lights*

*Kept by the Zandian*

*The Hand of Vengeance*

*Her Alien Masters*

**Regency**

*The Darlington Incident*

*Humbled*

*The Reddington Scandal*

*The Westerfield Affair*

*Pleasing the Colonel*

**Western**

*His Little Lapis*

*The Devil of Whiskey Row*

*The Outlaw's Bride*

**Medieval**

*Mercenary*

*Medieval Discipline*

*Lords and Ladies*

*The Knight's Prisoner*

*Betrothed*

*Held for Ransom*

*The Knight's Seduction*

*The Conquered Brides (5 book box set)*

**Renaissance**

*Renaissance Discipline*

**Ageplay**

*Stepbrother's Rules*

*Her Hollywood Daddy*

*His Little Lapis*

*Black Light: Valentine's Roulette (Broken)*

**BDSM under the name Darling Adams**

**Medical Play**

*Yes, Doctor*

**Master/Slave**

*Punishing Portia*

Printed in Great Britain
by Amazon